The American Earl

Joan Wolf

D1617422

Untreed
Reads

The American Earl
By Joan Wolf

Copyright 2020 by Joan Wolf
Cover Copyright 2020 by Untreed Reads Publishing

Cover Design by Ginny Glass

ISBN-13: 978-1-94913-566-4

Published by Untreed Reads, LLC
506 Kansas Street, San Francisco, CA 94107
www.untreedreads.com

Printed in the United States of America.

Publisher's Note

Chapter One

For as long as I live, I will never forget the morning I found my father's body. I had awakened with the dawn and decided to take a walk in the garden before breakfast. I wrapped my old wool cloak around my nightdress, slid my feet into my boots and went quietly down the stairs.

The French doors at the back of the house let me out into a beautiful morning. The air smelled frosty and clean and the moon was still bright in the sky. I began to walk along one of the pathways, thinking it was a perfect day for hunting and wishing we were going out. I was looking up at the moon when I stumbled over something on the ground. I gained my balance and looked down. Two legs wearing riding boots jutted out from the shrubbery.

My first thought was that some drunk had found his way into the garden and passed out. My second thought, as I regarded the expensive boots, was, if this is Papa, I'll kill him.

I dropped to my knees and pushed away the branches. A man was lying on his back in the midst of a tangle of boxwood. His face was a bloody pulp and I screamed. As I backed away from the ghastly sight, I saw the distinctive ring of the earls of Althorpe on the hand that was still clasping a revolver.

It was my father.

Nausea rose in my throat and I heaved the contents of what had been last night's dinner into the shrubbery. When I finally stopped retching, I ran for the stables, my cloak streaming out behind me.

Toby, the old groom who had known me all my life, was haying the horses. He took one look at my face, put his hands on my shoulders and pushed me to sit on an unopened bale.

"What's wrong, lass?" he said sharply. "You look as if you've seen a ghost."

"Toby, Pa...." I stuttered trying to get the words out, "Papa's dead. I found him in the garden. He...he killed himself."

My stomach heaved again, and I pinched my lips closed and swallowed hard.

Toby swore. Then he took my hands into his large, calloused warm ones. I was shivering and his hands felt good on mine.

He said, "What were you doin' out in yer nightdress anyway, lass?"

"I don't know." My teeth were chattering now. "I just wanted to go out into the morning. Then I found him." I looked up into my friend's weathered brown face. "What should I do?"

"You're sure he's dead?"

I shut my eyes. "Yes. His face was blown away, but I recognized his ring."

Toby swore and I opened my eyes. I had never seen him look so grim. "Go back to the house and get dressed," he said. I'll take Baron and ride to fetch Sir John."

Sir John Barrington was the local magistrate. I clutched my cloak around me and shivered some more. "What will he do?" I asked.

"He'll take care of things. Just you go back to the house, Lady Julia, and have a hot cup of tea."

"I'll have to tell Maria and Cousin Flora," I said, my voice quivering.

"You will," Toby said, that grim look still on his face. Then, as if he couldn't hold the words back any longer, "God in Heaven. What was the bloody man thinkin', to do such a thing to you? If he had to kill himself why didn't he do it somewhere else?"

"I d-don't know."

I let him pull me to my feet. The shock was receding a little and Toby's anger was igniting in me as well. "He always was a bastard," I said.

We looked at each other for a long moment, the truth clear and bleak between us. Then I said, "I'll go back to the house."

Toby patted my shoulder. "Tell me exactly where you found him, so I can tell Sir John. You don't want to see him again."

The dreadful picture of my dead father flashed before my eyes and I shuddered. "No."

I told Toby where to look and began to walk toward the stable door. My legs felt rubbery and I tried to steady my breathing.

"I'll have Sir John come to the house to speak to you after...when he's done," Toby said.

I nodded, went out the door and slowly made my way back to the house.

*

I let myself in the front door and walked along the passage that led to the family wing. Stoverton was really two houses, the grand fortified castle that had been built hundreds of years ago and the newer part, which had been built by my grandfather, where the family lived. The passage between the two wings was lined with high windows that showed a fountain on one side and a statue of a mostly naked Greek goddess on the other.

I went immediately to the library, my favorite room. From floor to ceiling the walls were lined with mahogany bookshelves filled with the books my family had collected over the years. The room was furnished with several Turkish rugs, two large desks, a globe, and a pair of ancient-looking but comfortable velvet sofas, which were arranged in front of the stone fireplace.

The room was cold. We never lit a fire in here until after breakfast. It was, in fact, one of the few rooms where we ever lit a fire. Coal was expensive.

I asked Lucy, our only maid, if she would ask Cousin Flora and my sister to join me. It wasn't long before they came into the room, both of them swathed in heavy shawls. I still wore my cloak draped over my nightdress.

Cousin Flora frowned when she saw me. "Julia, what on earth are you doing downstairs dressed like that?"

Flora was a short, stout woman with a kind face. She had come to stay with Maria and me a year ago, when Maria's governess was let go. She was one of my father's many cousins and my Aunt Barbara had invited (or pressured) her into living with us so there would be an adult female in the house.

Flora and Maria sat on the sofa facing me and I told them what I had discovered in the garden.

Maria went pale as snow. "Papa killed himself?"

"I'm afraid so." I went to sit beside her on the sofa and put an arm around her shoulders. Maria was four years younger than I and I had always taken care of her.

Flora said, her voice trembling, "Dearest Julia. What a terrible thing for you to find."

I nodded, unable to speak. Once again my stomach heaved and I gritted my teeth and forced it down.

Maria turned to look at me. She had been born with the famous good looks of the Marshalls. Her hair was golden, her eyes deeply blue, her features classically beautiful. There were tears in her eyes now, but I knew they weren't tears of grief. She was afraid of what Papa's death would mean for us.

"We'll be all right," I said. I was eighteen and had been in charge of Stoverton for several years. "I'll take care of you, Maria. Don't worry; we'll be all right."

Her mouth trembled but she nodded.

Neither of us felt any of the grief that one would expect to find in the children of a suddenly deceased father. We knew little about him and what we knew we didn't like. Maria put her head on my shoulder and whispered, "Oh Julia, what are we going to do?"

*

Sir John Barrington, the magistrate, had Papa's body removed to the icehouse. Then he met with Cousin Flora and me and asked if we had found a suicide note.

I hadn't even thought to look.

It was lying on the mantle in the morning room, propped up against a clock. My name was on the outside. Sir John, a stocky, brown-eyed man, handed it to me. I scanned it, gritted my teeth and handed it back to him.

The magistrate looked at me inquiringly and I said, "Read it so Cousin Flora can hear it too."

Sir John cleared his throat and began,

> *My dearest Julia, I am sorry to leave you and your sister this way, but it is for the best. My financial choices have made it impossible for me to provide for you. Tommy's boy will be the next earl, and I have looked into his situation. He is a wealthy man and I know he will do his duty by you. Believe me, this is the best solution for you and your sister. Your father, Philip, Earl of Althorpe.*

"Best solution," I repeated furiously. "The bastard!"

"Julia!" Cousin Flora bleated. "My young cousin is upset," she said to the magistrate apologetically.

"I understand." The brown eyes regarding me were kind. "There will have to be an inquest, Lady Julia, but I have seen enough to give evidence. You may bury your father whenever you please."

Cousin Flora moaned. "Oh dear. What are we to do about a burial, Sir John? Althorpe's a suicide. He can't be buried in consecrated ground."

"He should be buried at the crossroads with a stake through his heart." I said.

"You don't mean that, Julia!" Cousin Flora looked at me in distress. "You know you don't."

In fact, I did, but I realized the great scandal a suicide in the family would create. Centuries of Marshalls had made our name one of the greatest in England. I wouldn't let Papa's death tarnish my heritage.

I said to Sir John, "Is there any way to hide the fact that he was a suicide?"

He sighed. "I'm afraid not, Lady Julia. If it was only I who viewed the body, perhaps we might, but I brought several other men with me. I cannot guarantee their silence."

I clenched my fists at my side but said nothing. There was nothing I could say. My father would be buried in unconsecrated ground and the Marshall name would be stained forever by his cowardly action.

Cousin Flora said, "We must send for Lady Barbara, Julia. If anyone can make the rector bury Althorpe in the church, it will be she."

My Aunt Barbara was my father's younger sister and she had inherited all the ambition and determination that had passed him by. I disliked her intensely, but as I gazed into Flora's washed-out blue eyes, I realized that she was right. Much as I abhorred the idea, Aunt Barbara was our only hope.

Feeling desperate, I asked my cousin, "Will you write to her?"

"Of course I will, dear," Flora replied.

I gave her a grateful smile.

Sir John said, "What do you know about the next earl? Didn't his father go to America years ago?"

"Yes, he did," Flora said. "And according to Althorpe he must have done very well for himself. What a blessing that will be."

"Good God," I said out loud, the horror I felt clear in my voice. "Are you saying the new earl is an American?"

Chapter Two

I had sent Maria upstairs while Flora and I spoke to Sir John, and after he was gone I went up to her room. She was sitting in front of her cold fireplace wrapped in a blanket. I went to take the other chair and wrapped myself in an old wool shawl.

"What did Sir John say?" she asked when we were both as comfortable as was possible in this freezing room.

I told her about the problem of the burial and that Flora had sent for Aunt Barbara.

"You actually *invited* Aunt Barbara to come here?" Maria asked in amazement.

I sighed. "We need her to persuade the vicar to bury Papa in the church. She'll bully him into it and no one else can."

Maria's lips twitched in a small smile. "Yes, she will." Her face became grave again. "Who will be the new earl, Julia? Do you know?"

It may seem strange that we didn't already have this information, but after my brother Philip died, everyone had expected my father to marry again and produce a new heir. In this, as in everything else, he had been a disappointment.

When I didn't answer immediately, she asked, "Will we have to move out of Stoverton?"

Leave Stoverton? *Never!* I thought. I loved Stoverton more than anything in the world, except Maria. The Marshalls had lived on this land since the fourteenth century. I was *rooted* here in a way that my father had never been. I never wanted to leave.

I said somberly, "The new earl is the son of Papa's younger brother who went to America. The new earl is an American, Maria."

Maria's hand flew to her mouth. "But Julia—the Americans killed Philip!"

My brother had died when the yacht he was a passenger on collided with an American privateer in the Channel. It's true we

7

were at war with America, but that an American ship should dare come into English waters was almost unbelievable. Philip and the others on board had been thrown into the water and drowned. Since our other brother, Charles, had died a few years earlier, the earldom, according to British law, would pass to Papa's only brother. As he was dead as well, the earldom would go to the next nearest male Marshall, Thomas' son, who was an American.

The two of us sat there and contemplated the catastrophe that My father's suicide had brought upon us.

*

My father's funeral was quiet. Aunt Barbara had successfully bullied the vicar into allowing him to be buried in the church with all his illustrious ancestors, an honor which he most certainly did not deserve. None of our large extended family attended, nor did any of the tenants or villagers. The general feeling among family and dependents was the quicker my father was dispensed with the better.

My father's solicitor, Mr. John Shields, who bore a strong resemblance to a bulldog the squire once had, called on us the day after the funeral. Aunt Barbara, Maria and I met with him in the library. Since my aunt had arrived we had been forced to use more coal—I didn't want her to know how tight money was—so the beautiful old library looked warm and inviting as we sat in front of the large stone fireplace.

"There is nothing we can do about the estate until we hear from the heir," Mr. Shields said, after he had offered his condolences. "No creditors can be paid, no moneys dispensed."

Aunt Barbara and I were sitting on one of the old blue velvet sofas and the solicitor sat on the other one, facing us. He continued, "Lady Julia, I fear this means you won't have the allowance your father made you to run the house. My hands are bound. All of your father's estate is untouchable until we can speak to Mr. Evan Marshall, the new earl, and receive his directions."

8

Aunt Barbara said in her well-bred, haughty voice, "Surely you can make *some* arrangements, Shields. We're at war with America. How on earth are we to contact Evan Marshall if we can't get a letter to him?"

The bulldog face nodded solemnly. "I understand your concern, my lady. Since it's not possible for a British ship to land on American soil, I will direct a letter informing the earl of his new honor to an English solicitor in Kingston, Jamaica. I have worked with him before and found him trustworthy. He will put the letter aboard a Jamaican vessel bound for Boston. American ports are open to Jamaican goods."

"Is that where Tommy's son lives, Shields?" Aunt Barbara asked. "Boston?"

"He lives in a town just north of Boston called Salem, my lady. I looked into the family when your nephew Philip died; I felt it was necessary to know something about the new heir. His name is Evan Marshall and he owns a very profitable shipping company."

"He's in trade." My aunt looked as if she had spied a rat. "Well, at least he's got money. He'll need it. I don't think Althorpe left him anything but debts."

I felt as if I was living a nightmare. At least my father had given me an allowance to run the house, even though it was a pittance. Now I was to get nothing until this American agreed to it? How were Maria and I supposed to live?

Aunt Barbara thought she had the solution to this problem and after Mr. Shields had left, she told Maria and me to pack our clothes. "You're coming back to Mereton with me. I always thought it was a disgrace that your father allowed you to remain here with no adequate supervision. It was horribly improper."

She had tried to get me to go and live with her once before, and I had refused. I refused again. "I won't leave Stoverton. Someone has to be here to look after it."

"Don't be ridiculous, Julia. You are seventeen years old. You cannot possibly 'look after' Stoverton. Nor can you be left here on your own."

"I'm eighteen," I corrected her, my voice matching the haughtiness of hers. "And who else has looked after Stoverton for all these years, do you think? Mama was rarely here and my father not much more."

"You have a steward," Aunt Barbara said. "It is his job to look after things, not yours."

"The last steward left two years ago," I said flatly. "I've been doing his job ever since."

My aunt stood and began pacing the room. "This whole situation is outrageous. I knew I should have insisted you come to me after your mother died." She stopped and glared. "But you carried on as if I was taking you to a house of torture. And Philip, weakling that he was, stood by you."

Maria's soft voice made itself heard. "Please don't argue. It's upsetting."

"Of course it's upsetting," Lady Barbara snapped. "That is precisely why you should not be here. But Julia insisted…."

I went over to take Aunt Barbara's seat next to my sister and picked up her hand. "Our aunt is right about one thing," I told her. "You should go to Mereton. I'm sure Aunt Barbara will get you a governess and a music teacher, and you'll have Lizzie to talk to. It would be the best thing for you, Maria."

Aunt Barbara backed me up. "Of course we'll get you a governess, Maria. I'm sure Flora has tried, but…well, best not to say anything more. And your cousin Elizabeth will be happy to have your company."

Maria sat up straight. She had the Marshall family height as well as its coloring. At fourteen, she was four inches taller than I. "I won't go without Julia."

Her blue eyes held mine steadily. Everyone always talked about how stubborn I was, but Maria wasn't far behind.

"I can't leave," I told her.

"I never thought you would."

The two of us looked at my aunt. I said, "If Cousin Flora stays with us, everything here will be perfectly proper. No one has questioned its propriety for the last few years, and I don't see why that should change. It's not as if my father was ever here."

Aunt Barbara and I went back and forth for another half an hour on this topic, but, since she couldn't tie me up and carry me out of the house, I won. As she swept out in high dudgeon to return to her own respectable household, her final words were: "When you're hungry enough, send me word and I'll come and get you."

"She doesn't really want me," I said to Maria. "She'd take you happily, but she and I dislike each other intensely."

"I didn't want to go either," Maria said.

"Are you certain?" I asked, looking intently into her eyes.

"Yes." Maria grinned. "You're much more fun than Aunt Barbara, Julia."

I laughed and hugged her, but the thought of Aunt Barbara's last words was chilling. Where was I to find enough money for us to live on?

Chapter Three

I imposed an even stricter regimen than we had been following. We cut further back on coal consumption and went to bed early to save on candles.

Sir William Hartly, our Master of Fox Hounds and my best friend, sent us hams and haunches of venison. Maria kept chickens so we could have eggs. We were cold and often hungry, but we were still at Stoverton.

Then, two months after my father died, I received a visit from Mr. Shields. We sat in the library and he told me he had thought further about our situation and decided it would be appropriate to advance me an allowance from what was left in Papa's personal account.

I was hugely surprised. He had made such a point of not being able to do anything until he heard from the new earl. When I queried him on this, he looked uncomfortable.

"I...er...decided that the earl would not like it if his cousins were left penniless and the house was not attended to. Isn't a munificent amount, Lady Julia, but it will enable you to remain here at Stoverton with a degree of comfort."

"How much?" I asked baldly.

When he told me, I blinked. "That's much more money than the allowance I received from my father. Are you certain about this, Mr. Shields?"

He got that uncomfortable look on his face again and said that yes, he was certain. And he gave me the allowance money for the last two months as well as the next one!

When I imparted this news to Maria and Flora, they were ecstatic. Truthfully, I had been afraid that Flora wasn't going to stick it out with us, and if she left I didn't know what would happen. Without Flora, Aunt Barbara would have legal cause to remove us—and I knew she would use it.

But now I could buy enough coal to heat several rooms in the house and Mrs. Pierce, our cook, could order food from the grocer in town. Maria and Flora were happy, and I was ecstatic. I hoped the new earl would never come.

*

On April 11 Napoleon abdicated and the war with France was over. The war with America dragged on, however, and still we didn't hear from Evan Marshall. In August, we learned that negotiations for a peace treaty between Great Britain and the United States had begun in Ghent. Part of me was happy that no more men would be killed, but I must admit that part of me regretted the ending of a war that suited my purposes so well.

In November, the negotiators in Ghent announced they were close to an agreement. Shortly after this notice appeared in the papers, Mr. Shields drove out to Stoverton bringing with him the inevitable but unwelcome news.

I had just come back from a most satisfactory hunt and was still in my riding clothes when the solicitor's coach pulled up at our front door. I invited him into the library, which was warm and comfortable thanks to the allowance he sent me faithfully every month. Maria and Cousin Flora were sitting at one of the two big desks doing schoolwork when we came in; I couldn't see the point of heating the schoolroom when they could work in here. I used the other desk to keep the household accounts.

"Come and sit by the fire," I invited the solicitor. It was a cold, damp day and the poor man looked frozen.

"Goodness," Cousin Flora said, coming to greet the visitor. "What brings you here on such an ugly day, Mr. Shields?"

"I have received a letter from the new earl," he said, going to stand in front of the fire and hold out his hands out to the heat.

I offered Mr. Shields some tea, delaying the dread moment for as long as I could. He accepted gratefully and I dashed off to the kitchen. Mrs. Pierce and Lucy, our only remaining maid, were sitting in front of the fire sewing when I came in. Lucy jumped up

14

to put the tea on and Mrs. Pierce opened the cupboards to see what she might offer a guest.

"Will you bring it, Lucy, when it's ready?" I asked.

"Of course, Lady Julia."

Lucy was Mrs. Pierce's granddaughter and I had taken her in when her mother ran off with a man from the village leaving the child behind. Lucy had been only nine when it happened, but I had told Mrs. Pierce that she could live at Stoverton. I solved the problem of my mother's certain disapproval by simply not telling her. My good deed had been rewarded because Mrs. Pierce was fiercely loyal to me and wouldn't think of leaving. Nor would Lucy. That's why we still had a cook and a maid.

I went back upstairs and announced that the tea was coming. Mr. Shields peeled himself away from the fire and came to sit on one of the sofas that flanked it. I sat next to him and gestured for Maria and Cousin Flora to join us.

We talked about the weather, always a favorite topic of the English, until Lucy came in with the tea tray.

Cousin Flora poured the tea and we all sat back, teacups in hand, and stared at Mr. Shields.

"Well?" I asked. "What did this Evan Marshall have to say?"

"He acknowledged that he had received my second letter and was planning to take ship from Boston. He expects to reach us sometime in February."

I didn't realize I had been holding my breath until I let it out. "Well, I suppose it's inevitable," I said glumly. "He has to come sometime."

Mr. Shields put his teacup on the table and looked at me. "There is something else I need to speak to you about, Lady Julia. I have been going over the late earl's finances, and I think that I should put you in possession of some information before the new earl arrives."

This sounded ominous.

Next Mr. Shields looked meaningfully at Maria then back to me. "Perhaps we could be private?"

I said, "Maria can listen to what you have to say, Mr. Shields."

"Are you sure, Julia?" Cousin Flora said nervously. Clearly she thought the report was ominous too.

"Do you want to stay?" I asked my sister. "It's obviously not good news."

She nodded definitively. "Yes. Whatever Mr. Shields has to say, it will affect me too."

I turned back to Mr. Shields and lifted an eyebrow.

The solicitor sighed. "Very well. First let me give you some information about the new earl. Evan Marshall is, as you know, the son of your father's younger brother, Thomas. Thomas went to America when he was quite young and did very well for himself. He settled first in Boston and then moved to Salem, a city on the Atlantic coast just north of Boston."

He took another sip of his tea.

Cousin Flora said, "I remember Tommy very well. A delightful boy."

Too bad it wasn't Tommy we were dealing with.

Mr. Shields said, "He did so well that when he died he left a shipping business worth millions of dollars to his two children, his son Evan and his daughter Frances."

My eyes nearly popped from my head. *"Millions?"*

"Yes, Lady Julia."

This was the first good news I had heard since finding my father.

Maria said, "Do you think he will want to live here, in England?"

"I don't know," Mr. Shields replied. "His letter was rather terse. I must say he didn't sound happy about his new title and responsibilities. These Americans, you know, are an independent lot."

These words cheered me immensely. If he didn't want to be an earl, then he'd go home, I thought. Perfect.

Mr. Shields cleared this throat. "Lady Julia, I regret that I must also tell you that your father's personal debts are far greater than any of us anticipated. In fact, he has left debts that—as far as I have calculated—amount to almost half a million pounds."

Maria gasped. Cousin Flora almost dropped her teacup. The three of us stared in horror at Mr. Shields.

He went on, his bulldog face looking immensely sad. "There is no money left in the estate account and very little in the earl's private banking account."

"Then where are you getting the money you have been sending me?" I demanded.

That peculiar look came over his face again. "I have taken it from what was left in his personal account."

Something about this didn't sound right, but I didn't want the allowance to stop so I dropped the subject.

Maria asked, her voice sounding breathless, "What is going to happen to us, Mr. Shields?"

He said, "That will be up to the new earl, Lady Maria. You and your sister are now under his guardianship."

"His guardianship?" I glared at the solicitor. "I'm eighteen years of age. I don't need a guardian."

He looked at me steadily. "Under the law, you do, Lady Julia. The earl will take the place of your father until you marry."

I was so agitated that I jumped to my feet and began to pace up and down the big room. "Did my father lose all this money gambling? How could that be possible? Why would people gamble with him when they must have known he was a pauper?"

"I don't know, Lady Julia." Poor Mr. Shields looked wretched. "I am going to suggest that the new earl get an accountant to go through all the accounts and credit demands to see if he can make sense of what has happened."

The new earl. He probably thinks he's walking into another fortune. What will he do when he discovers the truth?

Cousin Flora said, "The art in this house is worth a fortune, Mr. Shields. Could not some of it be sold?"

My immediate reaction was negative. Sell off our art? The fabulous collection of paintings my ancestors had acquired over the centuries? It was part of Stoverton, part of what made Stoverton the treasure it was.

I pinched my lips together to keep from protesting. I certainly hadn't any other suggestions to make.

Mr. Shields said, "The entail includes all of the house furnishings, Miss Remington. Stoverton and everything in it does not really belong to the earl, as you must know. He is only holding it in trust for the next generation. Even if he wanted to, the new earl could not sell any of the art or furniture or beautiful objects that belong to the house. He must keep them in trust for his son."

Relief surged through me that my home wasn't going to be denuded and I returned to the sofa. "So we must just wait for this American to arrive and see what he will do?"

"I am afraid so, Lady Julia," Mr. Shields agreed. He pulled at the roll of flesh on his chin and sighed. "I am afraid so."

Chapter Four

On December 24, 1814, the Treaty of Ghent was signed, officially ending the war between Great Britain and the United States. Six weeks later, I received a letter from Mr. Shields informing me that the new earl had arrived in London. The solicitor planned to bring him out to Stoverton in a week's time, so he suggested we prepare to receive him.

I read between the lines of this missive and realized I had better open up some more rooms before the earl arrived. The entire castle wing of the house had been shut up for years, but in the family wing I decided to open the drawing room, the large dining room, and the earl's bedroom. We had been living mainly in the morning room, the library and the small dining room since my allowance had started.

I delegated the cleaning, assigning one room to myself, one to Maria and one to Lucy. Mrs. Pierce cleaned all the precious dishes and silverware that hadn't been used since my mother's death, and she and I consulted on menus so she could order the proper food from the village. Cousin Flora tried to do something about our clothes.

I started in the drawing room by pulling the holland covers off the furniture and piling them in a corner. I had a dust rag in my hand but before I went to work I stopped to regard the picture that hung over the marble mantelpiece. It was a portrait of the first earl, Philip Marshall, who had been my hero since I was a child. He was one of Queen Elizabeth's favored courtiers, a soldier, a statesman and a poet. Looking at him now, with the Elizabethan ruff framing his handsome blond head and clear blue eyes, I smiled. In truth, I adored Philip Marshall. There was a book of his poetry in the library, and I knew it all by heart. It was he who had first turned Stoverton from a fortified manor into a magnificent country house.

It had always annoyed me that I hadn't inherited his coloring. Maria was a perfect Marshall: blue eyes, golden hair, tall and slender. I wasn't tall, my hair was black and my eyes gray. My mother always said I got my looks from her side of the family, and I had always thought it horribly unfair that I, who loved Stoverton more than anyone else, was the one who didn't look like a Marshall.

We worked like slaves and by the time the new earl was due to arrive I thought the rooms looked impressive enough to humble an American millionaire. The drawing room was particularly beautiful, with its marble fireplace, tall windows and magnificent gilt-framed mirror hanging over an Italian sideboard. I had dusted the painted ceiling, climbing a very high ladder to reach it. I had also dusted and polished all the furniture and arranged the chairs, which usually stood against the wall, in a circle before the fireplace, making the picture of the first earl the centerpiece of the room.

On the day the new earl and Mr. Shields were to arrive, Maria and I dressed in our best frocks. I had refused to spend the precious allowance money on clothes when there was so much else that needed work in the house and on the farms, so we didn't exactly present a picture of elegance. In fact, the only presentable dresses we owned were the ones that Aunt Barbara had ordered for Papa's funeral. We might have looked gloomy, but at least the dresses fit.

Mr. Shields and his companion arrived at Stoverton's front door a few minutes before noon. Lucy, dressed in a maid's uniform Mrs. Pierce had unearthed from somewhere, answered the door and brought them to the drawing room, where Maria, Cousin Flora and I had arranged ourselves to greet them.

My heart was hammering as the wide door opened and Lucy said, as she had been instructed, "His Lordship, the Earl of Althorpe and Mr. John Shields."

The American walked into the room and stopped in a shaft of sunlight from the window. I stared, utterly stunned by what I was seeing.

He was tall and broad-shouldered, his hair was a thick, silvery blond, his features were chiseled and his eyes a clear, absolute blue. He was the living image of the first earl, Philip Marshall, whose portrait hung over the mantelpiece. The only difference between them was that Philip's hair was a slightly darker blond.

We stood and he came forward to shake hands. I offered mine, looked up into those intensely blue eyes, and managed to mutter something I hoped was polite. My heart was racing. How could this be? How could this American be the living embodiment of my Philip?

He next offered his hand to Maria, who said, "But you're the image of the first earl! Look—his picture is hanging right over the fireplace."

She pointed and his eyes followed her finger. "See." Maria said. "The resemblance is amazing."

"It certainly is," he said slowly, staring at the picture. His voice was deep and crisp, his accent different from ours. "This was the first earl, you say?"

"Yes, Maria said. "He was a famous Elizabethan soldier and courtier. Queen Elizabeth loved him so much she made him an earl."

"It certainly is extraordinary," he said, not looking overly happy about the resemblance.

Cousin Flora said comfortably, "Come and sit down, my lord. I have sent for tea."

He seated himself on one of the elegant gilt chairs I had arranged. He was a big man and shifted a little on the seat, trying to make himself comfortable. His eyes were still on the portrait.

"It's like looking in a mirror." His thick silvery brows were drawn together. "It's a little unnerving, actually."

Cousin Flora said, "There has always been a strong likeness among the Marshalls. I remember that your father was blond and blue-eyed too."

"Yes, he was. And my sister is as well."

The American pulled his eyes away from the portrait and looked at Maria and me. His face was grave as he said, "I deeply regret the tragedy that has brought me to England, but I am pleased to meet my new cousins."

Maria smiled eagerly. "Thank you, my lord. We are happy to meet you as well."

He smiled back. The smile made him look even more spectacular. "My name is Evan, Maria." His eyes passed over the three of us, and his smile deepened. "Please, I beg of you, don't call me by a title. We don't believe in aristocracy at home and it makes me extremely uncomfortable."

This could be good news. If he didn't like aristocracy he wouldn't want to remain in England for very long.

"Would you gentlemen care for a light luncheon?" Cousin Flora asked the earl and solicitor. "We are ready to serve if it pleases you."

"It pleases me very much. I'm starving," the earl said, gracing us once more with a smile. I suspected he got a lot of use out of that smile, but it didn't impress me. He was still an American, a citizen of the country that had killed my brother—who should be the one inheriting Stoverton instead of this interloper.

I led everyone into the small dining room where the table had been set with the two-hundred-year-old silver, and the Sevres china a countess had brought back from France during the reign of Louis the Fifteenth. I had ordered the best we had quite deliberately. I wanted this American to know what it was like to have such beautiful old things.

Lucy brought out a fish soup and we all lifted our spoons.

The meal was pleasant enough. I couldn't be openly rude and call the American by his title since he had asked us not to, so I didn't call him anything. Maria, on the other hand, chattered away, using his Christian name with as much freedom as if she had known him forever.

While Maria asked the earl questions about America and Cousin Flora asked questions about his father, I asked Mr. Shields if he had told the earl about our financial situation.

"I've told him there are large debts that need to be paid, Lady Julia. We won't know the full story until we have a chance to see what Stoverton is costing. Perhaps you should take him on a tour of the house and property. I'm sure he has no idea of the size of the estate. He comes from a small town that makes its livelihood from the sea."

I thought this was a good idea and when I suggested the tour at the end of the meal, Cousin Flora gushed, "You couldn't have a better guide than Julia, Evan. She knows everything there is to know about Stoverton and the family."

"How nice." He gave me an inscrutable look, which annoyed me as much as his smile did.

"May I come too?" Maria asked eagerly.

She got the smile. "I would be delighted if you would come, Maria."

A return smile lit her face. Maria was always grateful for attention. She had certainly never gotten any from our parents.

Cousin Flora said to Mr. Shields, "Perhaps you and I might take tea in the drawing room, Mr. Shields, while the tour is in progress?"

"That sounds lovely, Miss Remington," he replied. We left our empty pudding plates on the table and went out.

*

We started the tour in the courtyard in front of the original house. "I'm afraid I can't tell you Stoverton is an architectural masterpiece, my lord," I began.

"Julia." There was a note of danger in his voice. "Don't call me that."

"In this country you should expect to be called by your title."

"You're my cousin. I would like it if you would call me Evan."

23

I forced a smile. "Of course." I turned back to the house. "As I was saying, Stoverton was originally a manor house, but King Henry VII gave my ancestor permission to fortify it; the front you are looking at is that house. We no longer use it, but it is still very beautiful."

The three of us stood silent, looking at the lovely golden stone that seemed to glow in the thin winter sunshine. I drew the American's attention to the square castellated tower that was separate from the main house. "The building on your left is the King's Tower. Unfortunately, it's the only tower left from the original fortifications. You can still see what's left of the original wall, however." I indicated the crenellated stonewall that stretched halfway from the King's Tower to the house. "The wall, which used to surround the house, was punctuated by eight towers. Unfortunately only the King's Tower remains today."

The American said slowly, "It's so strange to know that my father grew up here. He never spoke about his English background. My sister and I didn't even know we had relatives over here, so you can imagine how astonished I was to receive the communication from Mr. Shields telling me I was the heir."

Maria was amazed. "Your father never told you about us?"

"No. He was an American, through and through. He even fought against England in the War of Independence."

What kind of a man would take up arms against the country of his birth? I held my tongue, but with difficulty.

Maria pointed to the structure that lay beyond the King's Tower. It was built in the same golden stone as the house, but in the Georgian style.

Maria said, "Those are the new stables. They were built by our grandfather."

Evan's blue eyes widened as he took in the size of the stable. "Great heavens! How many horses do you have here?"

"Only six," I said, and cleared my throat so he wouldn't hear the pain I always felt when I thought of all my beautiful horses sold to people who wouldn't love them like I did. "We have my mare, my father's old hunter, and four elderly carriage horses."

He threw me a quick glance, but I maintained a stoic face.

"I see."

Maria said, "Julia and I used to have a pony. Her name was Feathers and she taught both Julia and me to ride. When Papa sold her Julia and I were heartbroken."

She looked at me. "Weren't we Julia?"

I clenched my teeth and said nothing. I had wanted to kill my father when he sold Feathers.

Evan said, "Can we go into the house now?"

Grateful for the change of topic, I nodded and said, "Of course. First I'll show you the state rooms in the old house. They have been closed up for some years now. My mother occasionally used them to throw grand house parties, but after she died, we didn't need them anymore. I think you will like to see them, however."

We started with the drawing room, which had been added to the original house in the fifteenth century. Unfortunately, all of the furniture was swathed in holland covers, but the room's beautiful proportions were still visible. Next we passed into the huge formal dining room and thence to the bedroom apartments, where kings had slept. Even though the furniture was covered, the great glory of Stoverton—its vast collection of paintings—were enough to impress even the most ignorant colonial. The paintings were usually covered too, but I had removed the protective linens because I wanted the American to see what magnificence he had inherited.

We looked at the Titian "Portrait of a Young Man," a self-portrait of Rembrandt, a collection of Holbein portraits and many beautiful landscapes by Poussin, Watteau and Claude. We also had a Holy Family painted by Raphael, which was priceless. Small bronze statues were displayed on tables. My favorite was the equestrian statue by Bernini.

As we left the last room and approached the long gallery, the earl said, "We don't have as many valuable paintings in all of America as you have in just this one house."

I stared at him. He had sounded disapproving!

The long gallery was next, my favorite place in the old part of the house. It was a long open room, and its walls of delicate chestnut-brown paneling were lined with portraits of the Marshall family and their friends. My mother used to use it as a ballroom.

There were portraits of blond-haired earls, family portraits of mothers with children, equestrian portraits, portraits with dogs, even a portrait of a haughty looking woman holding a parrot.

My favorite portrait of all was a picture of the first earl's dear friend, Sir Philip Sidney. The two Philips had been very close – the first earl had even been at the Battle of Zutphen with Sidney when he was killed. Our Philip had stayed beside Sidney until he died of infection from his wounds, and he had accompanied the body home to England.

Philip Marshall had written poetry too—all of those Elizabethan soldier-courtiers seem to have been poets—but Sidney, of course, was the one whose poetry had become a part of our literary heritage.

The earl was attentive as I told him who was the subject of each of the portraits. When we had finally finished and were walking back along the passageway that connected the two main wings of the house, he said to me, "Mr. Shields wishes to go over the financials of the estate with me. I understand that your father left a large number of personal debts."

"I'm afraid that he did."

He stopped walking and turned to me. He was so big that my head reached only to his shoulder. He said, "I understand that you have been running the estate since before your father died. I hope you will consent to sit in on this discussion."

I was surprised by the request and said quickly, "I would like that very much."

"Good."

Maria was shivering and I told her to go on back to the library to get warm. "We don't heat this part of the house," I said.

"No use heating a house you don't use," he said practically.

"I suppose so. But it's not good for the paintings to be exposed to the cold like this."

He looked amused and I said stiffly, "I will have our maid show you to your bedroom. Don't worry, it has a fire."

His amusement deepened. "Julia, I live in Massachusetts. Nothing you have here in your small island can be colder than what I'm accustomed to at home."

Maria said eagerly, "I'll show Evan to his room, Julia."

She likes him, I thought. That smile has won her over.

Well, it hadn't won me. *Small island, indeed.* I thought. And watched Maria walk beside the earl, chatting comfortably, as they went toward the stairs that led to the upstairs bedrooms.

Chapter Five

Mrs. Pierce was an excellent cook and for dinner she produced roast mutton with roasted vegetables and potatoes that melted in your mouth. The soup was a repeat of the fish soup from lunch and was exquisite.

Evan—I supposed I had to learn to call him that—ate with gusto. We talked for a while about the weather, always a safe topic, and when that petered out, Evan asked Maria where she went to school.

"School?" Maria was understandably surprised. No Marshall girl had ever gone away to school. "I study at home," she explained. "I had a governess when I left the nursery, then, when Papa couldn't pay her any more, Julia taught me. But the family decided I needed someone older, and Cousin Flora came."

'The family' was my Aunt Barbara, who was always trying to stick her nose into our business. She had looked around for the poorest relation she could find and persuaded Cousin Flora to come. It's not that I didn't like Flora. She was always so pleasant it wasn't possible not to like her. But I knew I did a better job of teaching than she did.

"It's a good thing I did come," Flora said to Evan. "Julia's ideas of subjects suitable for a young girl were hardly appropriate." She shot me a reproachful glance. We had had this discussion before. "Nor were they subjects Julia herself should know anything about," Flora concluded.

Evan turned to me, his blue eyes curious. "What were you teaching that was so unsuitable?"

I had a mouthful of potato and couldn't speak, so Flora answered. "For one thing, she was teaching Maria what I can only consider to be warm stories from some old Greek books she found in the library." She gave me the reproachful look again. "Julia's governess failed to monitor her reading material, but she cannot be allowed to pass these indelicate tales along to her impressionable sister."

Evan's eyes glinted with curiosity and he asked Maria, "What 'old Greek books' did Julia teach you?"

"Homer, Sophocles, Euripides. We started to read Plato, but Cousin Flora took it away and hid it," Maria said sadly.

"Did you like those books?"

"Yes, I did!" Maria's voice took on a note of enthusiasm. "There was one particular story where this man has a prophecy that he'll marry his mother…"

"Stop!" Flora cried in horror.

Evan grinned. *"Oedipus Rex.* I had to read it in translation since I never learned classical Greek."

"We have some good ones in the library."

Maria put down her water glass. "Julia's always reading—that is when she isn't at the stables or riding."

Flora lifted her double chin. "I regret having to say this, Evan, but these girls have been neglected for years. Neither of their parents took the slightest interest in their educations. It's a disgrace the way they have been allowed to go on, with scarcely any supervision."

I said, "Maria and I did fine on our own, Cousin Flora."

"Not that we haven't liked having you with us," Maria added quickly. She had always been sensitive to the feelings of others. It was a great pity that my mother and father had never been sensitive to others.

Since our parents had scarcely ever come to Stoverton, I was the only person Maria could turn to for affection. I loved my sister deeply, but I understood she needed more than just me.

My plan was to get this American to do something for my sister. I glanced at him from under my lashes. I would never like him, but I needed his good will. I forced a smile and said, "Would you like to ride around the estate with me tomorrow, Evan? I can introduce you to some of our tenants."

He looked pleased. "I would like that very much."

I thought of the limited number of horses in our stable. The only one I could offer him was my father's old hunter, whose best days were long behind him. I explained this to Evan.

"A nice, solid old fellow will suit me just fine," he replied.

Lucy came in to remove the dinner dishes and I was relieved that Evan had made no comment upon our lack of male servants. A decent household would have had three footmen at least serving at the table.

Of course, they probably didn't have servants like that in the American wilderness.

Cousin Flora inquired, "Did you enjoy your tour of the house today, Evan?"

"I must confess I found it rather overwhelming. My whole house in Salem could fit into just a couple of rooms here in Stoverton."

"Do you have a house in the country as well as a town house?" Maria asked.

"No, just in Salem. That's where our shipping business is. My father settled in Boston when he first came to America, but then he moved to Salem and built his company there. It's a grand place to live. The whole town revolves around shipping."

"I remember your father from when we were children," Flora said fondly. "At Christmastime your grandfather always had a house party for all the family—aunts and uncles and dozens of cousins. It was so much fun! Tommy was always up to mischief— he had so much energy, that boy. I'm not surprised he made a great success in America."

I said, "It's strange how your father never mentioned his family in England, and my father never talked about your father either. I wonder why?"

His thick silver-blond brows drew together. "I don't know. The only person in England my father kept in communication with was an old school friend of his. They wrote fairly regularly."

The pudding came in, apple pie with a tiny bit of cream on top, and after we finished, Flora rose. Maria and I followed her lead. "We'll leave you to your glass of port," Flora said to Evan, who had stood along with us.

"But where are you going?"

"To the drawing room, to wait for you."

He looked bewildered. "I'm not supposed to come with you?"

I informed him, "In England the ladies retire after dinner and leave the gentlemen to their port."

Evan looked at me. His eyes were really amazingly blue. His resemblance to the portrait of the first earl was rather unsettling. "But why?" he asked. "In America the entire company retires to the parlor after dinner."

"I don't know why," I returned. "That's just the way it's always done."

Flora said, "If you'd like to have your port in the drawing room with us, Evan, come along."

"I don't like port," he replied, "and I'll be happy to join you."

The fire in the drawing room was still going so the room was pleasantly warm when we went in. I looked sadly at the empty spot in front of the hearth whereby dogs had always lain. Merlin, my last spaniel, had died just before I found my father and I hadn't replaced him. Once the business of Stoverton was settled, the first thing I would do would be to acquire some dogs.

We settled into the chairs that were still placed around the fire and Flora said, "Would you care for some music, Evan? Maria is a very good pianist."

"I would like that very much," he said, smiling at Maria.

The piano had originally been in the drawing room, but we had moved it into the library when we closed off so much of the house. Then we had dragged it back in here before Evan arrived. Maria had been so worried about its being out of tune from the moving that I had paid someone to tune it properly.

She stood up gracefully and went to take her place at the piano. She turned and said to Evan, "Is there anything particular you would like to hear?"

I waited to hear what he would reply. Did Americans know anything about real music?

"Something by Mozart would be wonderful – if that suits you, Maria."

My sister is an enormously gifted musician. She merely smiled back, turned to the piano, placed her fingers on the keys, and began to play.

I closed my eyes and listened. Maria usually played for Flora and me after dinner and it was the most peaceful part of my day."

When she had finished Evan said in surprise, "Where did you learn to play like that?"

"I used to have a piano teacher," Maria replied softly.

He frowned. "Used to? What happened to him?" Then, as Maria looked upset, he lifted his hand. "Don't bother answering. I can guess. Your father ran out of money."

Maria nodded. She looked so lovely sitting there, with her golden curls and her blue eyes and her black funeral dress. I felt a surge of fierce protectiveness.

"Of all of my father's transgressions, this was the worst." I said fiercely. "He *knew* how much music meant to Maria, but he didn't care."

"Well that is something I can easily rectify," Evan said. "When I get back to London I will look about for a music teacher for you, Maria."

The look of radiance on her face brought tears to my eyes. At that moment I almost liked Evan Marshall.

"Thank you, Evan." Maria's voice trembled with emotion.

He looked embarrassed. "It will be my honor," he replied.

It was the right answer for a Marshall. *Too bad he isn't English*, I found myself thinking.

He was speaking to me. "I understand that your father had two sons to succeed him. What happened to them?"

All my good feelings toward him died. I said in my most clipped voice, "My brother Charles died of a lung infection when he was young. Two years ago my brother Philip was sailing in the Channel with friends when a fog came down. His yacht was hit by an American privateer and all on board drowned."

Evan looked grave. "I'm so sorry."

"We heard that you were a ship's captain. Did you fight in the war?"

His blue eyes held mine steadily. "Yes, I did. I had my own ship, the Bonny Jean."

"So you were a privateer then, not in your country's navy?"

"Yes."

"Did you ever sail in the Channel?"

He replied in a level voice, "No. Most of my prizes came from the Caribbean."

My back was ramrod straight as I glared at him. "Those 'prizes' you speak of were non-combatant merchant ships, not ships of war. It was an act of cowardice to attack them."

"Julia!" I heard Flora say warningly.

Evan glared back at me.

"There wouldn't have been a war if your government had not continuously stopped American merchant ships and impressed our seaman – most of whom were American citizens – into your navy."

I opened my mouth to reply but he wasn't finished. "You may be upset that American ships were in the Channel, but your troops marched into Washington City—our country's capital—and burned it to the ground!"

I kept on glaring, furious that I couldn't think of anything to say. Then the fire in his eyes went out and he looked contrite. "I'm sorry, Julia. I'm sorry about your brother. Believe me, I would much rather it was he who was responsible for Stoverton than I."

I nodded and mumbled something indistinguishable in reply.

Cousin Flora said hurriedly, "What does your wife think about all this, Evan?"

"Not much, I'm afraid; I don't have a wife. I haven't been home long enough in the past few years to impress any girl."

I didn't believe him for a minute. He was a stunning looking man. The girls must have been all over him.

Cousin Flora's eyes widened. "Perhaps you will meet a girl in England who will take your fancy."

She shot a quick look at me.

Evan said, "I don't think so, ma'am."

I didn't think so either. What girl in her right mind would want to go and live in America?

Chapter Six

The following morning, Mr. Shields, Evan and I sat around the library desk where I kept the estate's accounts. Evan was dressed casually in a riding jacket and trousers, while I wore my usual house garb, an old blue wool dress that was both comfortable and warm. Mr. Shields was by far the best-dressed person in the room.

Mr. Shields opened the meeting. "I didn't get a chance to go over very much with you while you were in London, my lord, so I am afraid you will be unpleasantly surprised at what you are about to hear."

Evan said, "I'm sorry I was so short of time, but I was tied up with Mr. Adams, the American Minister. However, I've only to look around this house to guess that the earl didn't leave much in the way of money."

"You guess correctly, my lord. Let me apprise you of the situation."

Mr. Shields began to talk. I knew most of what he was going to say, but it was news to Evan. He was looking stunned by the time Mr. Shields finished.

He said, "Could no one have stopped my uncle from this destructive course?"

"Once his agent left, he was able to keep the amount of his debts a secret. My firm knew he was in trouble, but we never suspected anything as bad as this."

Disbelief was stark on Evan's face. "It's almost inconceivable to me that one man could go through so much money."

He was sitting directly in the shaft of thin winter sunlight coming through the window and I noticed how his hair shone like spun silver.

I still got a jolt when I looked at him, he was so like my Philip: the strong sculpted cheekbones, the straight nose, the firm mouth, the blue Marshall eyes. It was disconcerting, to say the least.

I dragged my attention back to the conversation. Evan was saying, "To sum up, the estate account, which should support the earl and his family, is empty, and my uncle has left personal debts of half a million pounds."

"Yes, my lord," Mr. Shields said. "I am sorry to break this news to you, but that is how your finances stand at the moment."

Evan turned to me, a thin line between his brows. "Julia, how have you been able to keep this house going if there were no funds available?"

"Mr. Shields has been sending me a monthly allowance from what was left in my father's personal account, which enabled me to pay for coal and groceries and give a salary to Mrs. Pierce, our cook, our maid, Lucy, and Toby, our groom. I was also able to buy hay and grain for the horses."

"Was there no one else in the Marshall family to come to your rescue? To take in you and Maria?"

This was a delicate question. Ignoring Aunt Barbara's offer, I said, "I'm afraid not. My father had borrowed from everyone, you see, and was exceedingly unpopular with the family."

His eyes narrowed. "Why should your father's behavior reflect upon you?"

Fortunately, Mr. Shields was anxious to get back to the main topic of our meeting. "In addition to his late lordship's personal debts there are several other demands on the estate I must mention, my lord."

"More debts?" Evan asked, his voice dangerously quiet.

Mr. Shields looked unhappy. "It's more like a failure of responsibility, my lord. The retired servants have not been receiving their pensions."

I felt stabbed to the heart. "Dear God, Mr. Shields. Nanny? William Coachman? Mrs. Henley, our old housekeeper? They haven't been getting their pensions?"

"I'm afraid not, Lady Julia."

Evan said, "You will have to explain this to me, Mr. Shields. The earl pays pensions to his servants when they retire?"

"All the great aristocratic families do so, my lord. Not every servant, of course, but people who have been with the family for almost an entire life-time receive a pension."

"So that is an additional cost upon the estate?"

"Yes, my lord."

"Why are they not able to save for their own old age?" Evan's voice was reasonable.

"They don't make enough money, my lord." Shields said.

Evan turned to me. "How much do you pay your servants, Julia?"

"Do you mean how much I am paying Cook and Lucy now, or how much should they be paid?

"How much is the usual sum to pay a servant in this country?"

I told him.

His eyes shot sapphire sparks. "I pay my cook and housekeeper three times that amount. And they get a quarter of a year's salary at Christmas. No wonder your servants can't save any money. They're paid like paupers!"

I flushed with anger. Who was this colonial to criticize us? "I can assure you that English servants are treated very well. They have their own rooms, new uniforms every year, and a half-day off a week!"

"If this was America you wouldn't be able to hire anyone under those conditions," he retorted.

"At least we pay them something! And they're free to leave when they want. We don't have slaves here, my lord, like you do in your precious country."

His face grew very grim. "Slavery exists mostly in the south, and we are working to get rid of it. I personally would never own a slave."

"Good for you," I said nastily.

Mr. Shields cleared his throat, and after a few seconds we broke eye contact and looked back at the solicitor. He said, "There is more than just the pensions to worry about, my lord."

Evan's jaw set. "Go on."

"I regret to tell you, my lord, that your late uncle also took the money that had been set aside for his daughter's dowries. Lady Julia and Lady Maria have been left with nothing."

Mr. Shields hadn't told me this. I looked down at the table and a chill ran down my spine. Maria and I had been *"left with nothing"*? My father had killed himself and thrown us on the mercy of this American he had never even met. If my father wasn't already dead, I would have killed him myself right there and then.

Evan avoided looking at me, which I appreciated. It's not easy to realize you are totally dependent on someone you don't even know. I put my hands in my lap and clenched them together.

Evan said, "So my uncle committed suicide because he couldn't see a way out of his financial problems and decided to dump them on me."

Neither Mr. Shields nor I said anything. The answer was obvious to us all.

"And I can't sell Stoverton because of this entail?"

"That is right my lord."

"Wonderful," Evan muttered. "What about all the paintings and the other priceless statues and stuff that Julia showed me. Can I sell them?"

"I am afraid not, my lord," Shields answered regretfully. "The entail includes the house and all its contents."

"What about selling off some of the land?"

I was almost breathless with terror as I answered, "The land is our only source of income, Evan! Any business shares Papa might have had are long gone. The money that comes in from the home farm as well as the tenants is what we have always lived on."

40

Mr. Shields backed me up. "Lady Julia is correct, my lord. The Marshalls have always been richer in land than in money, but the land has always enabled them to live comfortably up to the standards of their class."

Evan's frustration let itself out in a long release of air. "Is there nothing I can do to raise money?"

Mr. Shields' mouth curved in a thin smile. "There is some good news, my lord. The late earl never mortgaged Stoverton. I suggest you raise money by taking out a mortgage on the estate."

"A mortgage!" My voice squeaked in horror. "No Marshall would ever mortgage Stoverton! Not even Papa stooped as low as that."

Blue eyes bored into mine. "Then how do you suggest I find the money to pay off your father's debts, Julia?"

I stuck up my chin and said boldly, "You have a lot of money, Evan. Think of all those Caribbean prizes you stole from English merchants. You could use *them* to save Stoverton."

His eyes hardened. "I am rich, but when I invest my money, I expect to get a good return on it. I don't think that Stoverton will do that for me."

"Stoverton will be the best return you could ever get for your money!" I spoke with all the passion that was in me. "It's ancient, historic and beautiful. It's filled with the civilization of centuries. And it has been your family's home for five long centuries. Your roots are here, Evan. Surely that is worth more than an accumulation of money in the bank?"

"My roots aren't here, Julia," said this American usurper. "My roots are in Salem, Massachusetts. And when I spend money on a beautiful ship, I expect to earn money from that ship. And I do. I earn a great deal of money. Stoverton isn't going to earn me any money, it's only going to cost me."

He sounded like a cit, I thought disdainfully. A middle-class, money-grubbing cit.

I said, "Making money for its own sake is worth nothing. Money is only valuable if it gives you a quality of life worth living."

"I think my life is worth living, thank you," he said between his teeth.

"My lord, Lady Julia," Mr. Shields bleated. "Can we turn our thoughts back to the subject of our meeting?"

"Yes." Evan pushed back his chair as if he was about to rise. "I have opened an account at Barings Bank in London. I will authorize you to draw on it, Mr. Shields, to see that all of the pensions to retired servants are paid. Back to when they were stopped, of course. And hire some more servants. This enormous building needs more attention than it has been getting. Oh, and double the servants' usual wages. I am not the sort of man who takes advantage of the people who work for me."

He stood up and looked down at me. "I believe you were going to show me around the estate, Julia."

I looked at him standing there in all his male beauty, a perfect Marshall come to life, and I wished he would go back to America and never return to England again.

Chapter Seven

I changed clothes for my ride with Evan and told Toby to saddle up Baron with my father's old saddle. I threw my sidesaddle on Isabella and had just finished tightening the girth when Evan walked into the stable yard. He was dressed in the coat he had worn for the meeting and fawn colored riding breeches. The breeches were cut too loosely, and his boots were too short. He was a man who traveled on boats and was probably not much of a rider. I thought it was a good thing that Baron was old and quiet.

My own riding clothes weren't fashionable either, but I wasn't a millionaire. I wore a warm red wool jacket over the riding skirt that had seen me through many a hunt. My boots were old, but I kept them polished.

I introduced Toby to Evan and to Toby's great surprise, Evan shook his hand. Toby said, "This here is your horse, my lord. He's a good lad. You've nothing to worry about."

Clearly Toby had summed up Evan's riding ability the same way I had.

Evan walked up to Baron, patted his nose and said, "Hello there, fellow." Then he offered Baron some sugar.

"Where did you get that?" I asked.

"I stopped by the kitchen and asked for it. Mrs. Pierce unearthed some from a back cupboard." He smiled at Toby. "And you are in charge of the stables?"

"Taught Lady Julia to ride, I did," Toby replied proudly. "But don't let her tell you I'm in charge of the stable, my lord. Lady Julia runs things here. She has since she was just a mite."

"I can believe that," Evan said.

I gave him a suspicious look.

He walked around Baron and put his foot in the stirrup.

"Here, my lord, we have a mounting block," Toby said.

"That's all right," Evan replied and swung easily up into the saddle.

It was immediately apparent that the stirrups were too short, and he took his feet out of them and began to lengthen the leathers. Toby hurried to assist him.

I swung up into my own saddle and waited until Evan's stirrups had been adjusted to suit him. Then I nudged Isabella and began to walk away from the stable. As Evan joined me, I was surprised to see how comfortable he looked in the saddle. Perhaps he wasn't such a bad rider after all. I decided to take him first through the park, which stretched for miles behind the house.

"What a beautiful mare," Evan said, his eyes running over Isabella's satiny bay coat. "A Thoroughbred?"

"Yes." I adjusted the reins with my gloved fingers. "She was bred to race but wasn't fast enough. That's the reason I was able to get her. She's a wonderful hunter, though. She'll go over any jump no matter how wide or high it may be."

He looked surprised "You hunt?"

"Yes." I glanced at him. "How about you? Do you hunt, Evan?"

He gave me an easy smile. "We don't do much hunting in Massachusetts. We use horses to get us where we want to go. I did ride out with a hunt once, though, in Virginia. They're great horse lovers down there. They breed and race thoroughbreds, like you do over here."

"I love hunting more than anything," I confessed. "Did you like it?"

He shot me a rueful look. "I have never been so terrified in my life."

My eyes widened. The men I knew would never admit to being frightened. "Did you fall off?"

He laughed. "I was far too frightened to fall off. I just hung onto my horse's mane and prayed."

I pictured the scene in my mind and smiled.

He said, "My sister has hunted though. My brother in law is originally from Virginia and she's spent some time down there visiting. They don't usually let women hunt, but Frances is a determined woman. She loved it."

"Women don't usually hunt here either. Not seriously, at least. They dress up in riding habits and ride along for a mile or so. Then they go back home."

"But you're not like that," he said.

"No."

We had entered the park by now, with its rolling acres of grass and trees and bridle paths. We even had an ornamental lake.

I was curious about this sister of Evan's and asked, "Is your sister older than you or younger?"

"She's two years older. We were always close as children and now she's my partner in the shipping business."

"Partner? You mean she owns it with you?"

"Yes. And because I've been away so much, she's the one who runs it."

"By herself?"

"Her husband works with her. He's a smart man, John. I like him, even though he's from Virginia."

I look up at him, squinting a little in the sun. "How old are you, if you don't mind my asking."

"Not at all. I'm twenty-seven."

"Will you take up the business when you go home again?" I asked. "Or do you plan to remain in England?"

He looked horrified. "Let us be clear on this, Julia. I do not plan to remain in England. I'll do my best to straighten things out for you here, but then I'm going home."

To disguise my glee at this response, I said, "Let's give the horses a gallop to shake the stiffness out of them," and took off. I heard Baron's hoof beats right behind me and we galloped full out along the winding bridle path under the bare winter trees.

*

45

I took Evan over every inch of the twenty-eight thousand acres that comprise Stoverton. We went through the Home Woods and around the lake. We rode around the extensive farmlands and I introduced him to our tenant farmers and their families. I knew them all, knew the names of their children and the names of their cows and pigs as well. I had been visiting them since I first learned to ride, and they all knew how much I wished I could do something to help them.

Evan was friendly and courteous. Most of our tenants were polite but subdued. They didn't know what to expect from this strange American who now held the power of their livelihoods in his hands.

I explained to Evan as we rode back toward the house that most of our tenants had been farming Stoverton land for a long time. Some of the families had been here for centuries. It was the income from the farms that made up the bulk of our family's income.

He was quiet for a while, riding Baron on a loose rein as we walked along one of the bridle paths in the woods. I was just going to ask him what he was thinking when he spoke. "Those cottages. Do they belong to the tenants or to the estate?"

"They belong to the estate, like the land. The tenants pay us to rent them."

"Who is responsible for the upkeep of the tenant farms? The tenant or the landlord?"

I looked straight ahead, between Isabella's pointed ears. "The landlord," I said in a small voice.

"Those cottages are in wretched condition. I wouldn't house animals in them at home. How was this allowed to happen?"

"My father never put any money into the estate. He just took the rent money and gambled it away. Surely you got that picture from our meeting with Mr. Shields this morning."

He was silent. Finally I looked at him. "I haven't been collecting rents since my father died. The tenants need what they grow to feed their families."

"I know it's not your fault," he said. His profile looked set and stern and I thought he would be a hard man to cross." He glanced at me then went back to looking straight ahead. "I'm going to be honest with you, Julia. This inheritance is a burden I don't want. I tried to get out of it, but I can't. Under your law, I am the Earl of Althorpe and am responsible for the lives of people whom a few months ago I never knew existed."

"Dear Christ," he said, "The looks on the faces of those people! Those dreadful cottages!"

"I know." My voice was muffled. I was mortified but there was no excuse I could offer.

"Neglect like that must have started well before your father took over."

I looked between Isabella's ears and didn't reply.

The path narrowed and the horses splashed across a stream and scrambled up a small hillside. When we were again able to ride side by side he said, "Those cottages must be completely rebuilt. I can't have people who work for me living in squalor."

"It's hardly squalor," I protested weakly.

He shot me a scornful look. "American workers would never consent to live in such conditions. But American workers have choices about their employment. It seems this is not the case in England."

I hated this. I hated the way he kept comparing us to America. It was true that Papa, and my grandfather as well, had been poor custodians of their heritage, but the heritage was still here. Beautiful Stoverton, with its history and its magnificent collection of art, was still here. The spirit of Philip Marshall lived on in every golden stone, every part of the beautiful landscape he had created for his family and his heirs. I had to make Evan understand that beautiful things are worth preserving for their own sake.

47

I squared my shoulders and Isabella, anticipating being asked to trot, began to prance. I quieted her and asked, "What do you do with all the money that you make from your ships, Evan?"

He quirked an eyebrow, as if he didn't understand me, but he kept facing forward.

"Do you have a collection of beautiful paintings in your home? A library full of wonderful books? Do you have rooms that are filled with beautiful furniture?" I waved my hand indicating our surroundings. "Do you live in the midst of great natural beauty?"

He still hadn't turned to look at me and I continued to stare at his profile. "What do you spend your money on, Evan?"

I thought I saw a muscle jump in his jaw. "My father bought paintings and books," he said. But he sounded defensive.

"And what have you bought?"

"Ships."

"So you can earn more money?"

"Yes."

"Look around you," I said. We had come out of the woods onto the lawn and a small herd of deer was grazing under a clump of oak trees. The sun, which had gone under a cloud, slid once more into the deep blue sky and glinted on the spraying water of the fountain. In the distance the golden stone of Stoverton looked as much a part of the landscape as the deer and the trees and the stretching turf lawns.

I said, "Do you have vistas like this in Massachusetts?"

"We have the ocean at our door, and that is beauty enough for me," he returned.

He is a cit through and through, I thought, with a mixture of anger and frustration.

"Stoverton needs someone who loves it," I said.

"Like you?"

I lifted my chin. "Yes, like me."

He shook his head. "Even if the estate had been left to you, you wouldn't have the resources to save it, Julia. I didn't want this house, or these acres. I didn't want the responsibility of two young girls. But I've got it and I must do the best I can under the circumstances."

I said carefully, "You may be responsible for Maria, but I am eighteen and old enough to be my own mistress."

He turned to look at me. "Of course I'm responsible for you. You're my cousin, you're unmarried, and you have no money. What is to become of you if I don't make some arrangements for your future?"

"I will be perfectly happy to remain here at Stoverton to keep an eye on things for you." A brilliant thought struck me. "I could be your agent, Evan!" I rose a little in my stirrups to look taller. "There's the perfect solution for the both of us! You can order what repairs you feel are necessary and I will be here to make certain your orders are carried out!"

"You can't live by yourself in this huge house," he protested.

I could, of course, but I needed to sound cooperative. "I can always get someone to stay with me. That's not a problem."

"Somehow I don't think that would pass muster with the rest of your family."

It wouldn't, of course. But I had another thought. "You just told me your sister has been running your own business for years. If she can do that, why can't I run Stoverton?"

"Frances is married."

"What difference can that make?"

"A big difference, I'm afraid," he replied.

"But don't you see? It's a perfect solution to both our problems. You don't want to remain here and I do. We each are the answer to the other's desire."

"I'll think about it," Evan said.

He sounded doubtful but I knew I could convince him. The idea of Evan back in America and me in charge of Stoverton—after Evan had paid off all the debts, of course—was the perfect solution to my future. I was quite in charity with him as we rode our horses into the stable yard.

Chapter Eight

Evan was feeling grim as he walked to the house, leaving Julia behind at the stables to help Toby. It appeared that, along with her other responsibilities, Julia was also a groom.

The household here at Stoverton was impossible, Evan thought. How on earth could Julia believe he would leave her by herself to run this massive museum? She was eighteen years old, for God's sake. And Maria was fourteen. Not only did he have his uncle's debts to deal with, now he had to come up with a solution for his uncle's daughters!

He let himself into the house and headed for the library, where Maria and Flora were supposed to be doing schoolwork. He found them sitting together at one of the big desks, with books and paper spread out before them.

"I'm sorry to disturb you," he said, "but might I speak to you for a moment, Cousin Flora?"

"Certainly." Flora stood up. "Keep working on those French verbs Maria and I'll test you on them when I return."

Maria sighed. "Yes, Cousin Flora."

Flora followed Evan into the hallway. "Why don't we go into the morning room?" she suggested.

Evan followed her into the pretty room that looked out on the south lawn. A fire was burning in the fireplace and the chintz-covered furniture looked comfortable, if a bit worn. A few lesser masterpieces adorned the walls.

"Would you like tea?" Flora asked.

Evan would have liked some, but he didn't want to wait until Lucy had been sent for, and the tea made and brought up to them. So he shook his head and said quietly, "Flora, what can I do to help Julia and Maria?"

Flora's pale blue eyes filled with tears. "Their situation is so appalling, Evan. How their father could have left them like this is something I will never understand."

"I agree. But they have been left destitute, and clearly I must do something. I just don't know what it is. I will restore their dowries, of course. But will that fix the problem?"

Flora's face lit. "Will you really do that? Oh, bless you, Evan. It will help a great deal. If Julia has a decent dowry she can be presented to society and hope to catch a husband. That's the answer to the problem of Julia and Maria. Get Julia married and her husband can provide a home for Maria until she is old enough to find a husband for herself."

Evan sighed. "I don't think Julia wants a husband, Flora. In fact, she asked me if she could stay here and be my agent for Stoverton."

Flora threw up her hands. "Julia and Stoverton! Most young girls dream of marrying, but all Julia has ever wanted was to stay at Stoverton! She should be making her come out in society, like other girls of her age and station in life. Unfortunately, it was never talked about because there wasn't the money for it."

Evan frowned. "I don't understand why other members of the family haven't stepped in to help these girls. It's outrageous that they should have been abandoned like this."

"Your aunt, Lady Barbara Lewis, wanted them to live with her after their mother died, but Julia refused. She is completely undisciplined, Evan. She spends her time reading inappropriate books and hanging around the stables with that groom. Do you know who her best friend is, besides Toby?"

"Who?"

"The local squire, a man of almost sixty! The two of them spend hours together, working with the hounds and hobnobbing in the stable. It's disgraceful. She can't be allowed to go on this way."

"How could her mother have allowed this?"

"Her mother was rarely at Stoverton. Helen was a...worldly...woman, Evan. As soon as she married the late earl she established herself in the family mansion in Piccadilly and, over the years, she became one of the most influential hostesses in the *ton*. My sister and I were forever reading about her in the gossip sections of the London newspapers."

"The *ton*?" Evan raised one blond eyebrow in inquiry.

"That's the name given to the most fashionable level of English society."

"You don't sound as if you liked my aunt much." It was a statement, not a question.

"I didn't know her well enough to like or dislike her. Helen carried her head far too high to notice those of us who were beneath the distinction of her own elevated position in the world."

"I see," Evan said slowly. "What about my uncle? What did he do with himself, aside from gambling? It sure doesn't look as if he devoted much of his time to the estate."

"He had a position in the government to make him look important. Helen got it for him through one of her…connections."

This last word was spoken with a distinctly ironic tone. Evan decided it would be wiser not to ask any more questions about Julia's mother.

"I think you're right about getting Julia married. Do you have any suggestions as to how we can introduce her to some eligible young men?"

Flora replied decisively, "You must take her to London and give her a Season. That is how all the young girls of Julia's class meet husbands. She will go to balls, the theatre, the opera. Most important of all, she will go to Almack's. *That* is where young men and young women in search of a spouse go to meet each other."

A lock of hair had fallen over Evan's forehead and he pushed it back. "I can't take her to London, Flora. I don't know anyone here in England. That is something a mother should do."

Flora sighed again. "If Julia was a normal girl, we could find a well-connected woman to present her and take her around to all the parties. But Julia isn't a normal girl, Evan, and she would intimidate and dominate any poor woman you might hire to chaperone her."

"She's certainly different from the American girls I know," Evan said with a grin.

"She's different from other English girls too," Flora said. "If I might make a suggestion, I think should you speak to your aunt, Lady Barbara Lewis. She is bringing out her youngest daughter this year and hopefully you can persuade her to bring Julia out along with Elizabeth."

Evan brightened at the idea of having someone else take charge. "I've never met my aunt. In fact, I never knew I had an aunt until Mr. Shields told me. How should I go about contacting her?"

"She doesn't live far from here. You can easily drive over to Mereton."

"I'll do that." Evan frowned slightly. "Do you know, Cousin Flora, I'm finding it more and more strange that my father never mentioned his family in England. Did something happen to estrange him from them?"

Flora's eyes widened in surprise. "You don't know why he emigrated to America?"

Evan shrugged, his big shoulders moving easily under his too-loose coat. "He always said that England was stifling, that there wasn't room to grow there. He said that the English judged people by their class, not by their character or abilities. He loved America because it wasn't like that."

"Did you know that your mother was also English?"

"Of course. She and my father came to America together when they were very young. My grandmother came with them. My father always said it was the money she inherited from her father that enabled him to start his business."

"How very interesting." Flora tilted her head and regarded him. "You deserve to know the truth. Your mother is the reason why Tommy emigrated. She was the daughter of Stoverton's housekeeper, your grandmother. Emma and Tommy grew up together, but of course there was a huge class gap between them.

When Tommy told your grandfather that he wanted to marry Emma, your grandfather threw Emma and Emma's mother out of the house. Tommy followed them, married Emma, and took ship for America. The estrangement between his father and Tommy was permanent, and it seems to have extended to his brother and sister as well."

Evan was dumbfounded. He shook his head as if to clear it. "I never knew anything about my parents' life in England. I never knew my father was the son of an earl. It was as if life started for them when they landed in Boston. Both of them were staunch Americans."

"They had reason to be. Apparently America was very good to them."

"Yes, it was."

"How did your father die, Evan? I was fond of Tommy and I would like to know what happened to him."

A scene flashed through Evan's mind, himself standing in front of a roaring fire in the house on Chestnut Street, and Frank Hickey coming into the parlor to speak to him.

"I'm so sorry to have to tell you this, lad, but your mother ran out on Lacy's Pond to catch a dog the Webster children had let get loose, and she fell through the ice. Your Pa tried to save her, and he went under too. We can't even get to the place where it happened; the ice is too thin."

For a brief moment pain knifed through him. His parents had been in their forties and in excellent health. The news had been devastating for him and Frances. He had been eighteen and Frances two years older, and all of a sudden they were orphans and the owners of a large business.

He said in an expressionless voice, "Both my parents fell through the ice on one of our ponds and were drowned."

"Oh dear." Flora reached out to put a hand on his arm. "I am so sorry. That must have been very painful for you, Evan."

"Yes."

She patted his arm and sat back.

He said, "So you think I should pay a visit to my Aunt Barbara?"

"Yes. As I said, she is bringing out her own daughter this season, so she is perfectly placed to bring Julia out as well." Flora sighed. "However, you will have your work cut out in order to convince your aunt to do that for Julia."

He raised an eyebrow in inquiry.

"Lady Barbara does not like Julia. Nor does Julia like her aunt. That is the biggest problem. Another one is that the Lewis' will not wish to pay for Julia's expenses. They are well off, but the cost of presenting Elizabeth will be high. They will have to rent a house for the season, which is expensive." Flora leaned forward. "I think this will be your most potent bargaining point, Evan. Offer to let Lady Barbara use the Picadilly mansion in London to present both Elizabeth and Julia. She'll jump at the chance."

"Ah, yes. I've been told I have a London townhouse. Is it enormous and filled with priceless art, which I can't sell?"

Flora smiled at him. "You're a good man, Evan. The girls are very lucky that you are their father's heir."

Chapter Nine

The following morning Evan left Stoverton to pay a visit to his father's sister. He drove an old curricle from Stoverton hitched to two of the old carriage horses. Toby's nephew Sammy went along as his groom.

The roads in England were markedly better than the roads in America, and Evan accomplished the two-hour drive with little difficulty. He turned in through iron gates and drove up the winding drive. When the house came into view the midday sun was reflecting off its lovely old mellow stone and high windows. To complete the picture, the house was surrounded by a wide sweep of perfectly tended lawn.

Evan left Sammy holding the reins, advanced up the walkway to the front door, and rapped the knocker.

It was a disorienting feeling, this business of meeting a whole new family he had not known existed. Evan was beginning to feel as if his parents' life had been an iceberg, with a great portion of it kept hidden from their children.

A butler garbed in formal attire answered the door. Evan introduced himself and the butler took his hat and coat and escorted him to a formal drawing room. "Her ladyship will be with you shortly, my lord," the servant said.

Evan inquired about his groom and horse and was told they would be taken care of. The butler departed, leaving Evan alone in the coldly formal room. He looked around automatically for the paintings; the few that hung upon the walls were mostly landscapes. He wondered what Julia would say about them—were they good or were they mediocre? He himself had no idea.

Evan took a seat on one of the spectacularly uncomfortable French chairs that were placed in front of the marble fireplace and prepared to wait.

In a remarkably short time, a tall, handsome, blonde-haired woman came in the door. "Evan, my dear," Lady Barbara said as she crossed the pale ivory and blue rug to greet him. "How lovely to meet you."

He blinked as he stood up to greet her. She looked just like his father. "I am happy to meet you as well, Aunt," he replied, and bestowed a chaste kiss on the cheek she presented to him.

Lady Barbara looked up. "Goodness," she said. "You wear your lineage on your face, Nephew. You are all Marshall."

Evan thought of the portrait hanging in the drawing room at Stoverton and of his shock when he had first beheld it. "So it seems," he said mildly.

Lady Barbara bade him be seated and once again Evan took one of the uncomfortable silk-covered chairs.

She sat beside him. "I'm sorry my husband isn't here to greet you, but he has gone to visit his brother. If he had known you were coming, he most certainly would have remained at home. The family has been eagerly awaiting your arrival." She looked at him piercingly. "I imagine you have learned by now of the disaster Philip left behind when he shot himself."

She didn't even wince when she mentioned her brother's suicide.

"Yes," Evan said, looking into the familiar yet strange face next to him. He decided to be honest and added wryly, "I must confess I'm finding it a bit disconcerting to meet relatives I didn't know I possessed. My parents brought me up to be one hundred percent American, you see. My father maintained no connection to his English family—it was as if they didn't exist. So you can imagine how stunned I was to receive a letter informing me that I was the new Earl of Althorpe—with all the attendant obligations."

He couldn't quite keep the bitterness out of his voice as he pronounced the last words.

Lady Barbara sighed. "I'm afraid that my father and yours quarreled badly, my dear. Do you know the reason why your father emigrated to America in the first place?"

"I recently learned the history of my parents from Cousin Flora," he replied steadily.

"Then you will know that my father was outraged when Tommy eloped with Emma. I was only a schoolgirl, but I can still remember his anger. He said that Tommy was no longer his son and that he had made his bed and he could lie in it."

"Nice of him," Evan commented dryly.

"Tommy was Papa's favorite," Lady Barbara said. "He felt that Tommy had betrayed him and his family by marrying so far beneath his station."

I'm glad I never knew the old bastard. Evan thought. Maybe it's poetic justice that my mother's son is the one to inherit his precious earldom.

Lady Barbara was going on, "Apparently Tommy did quite well for himself in America."

"Let us just say that my father was wiser with his money than my uncle was with his," Evan said.

At this point, the butler came in with a tea tray. A table was set up in front of the chairs and Lady Barbara asked Evan polite questions about his journey from America while she poured. When the butler closed the door again, she got down to business. "I know my brother was deeply in debt. How bad is it?"

Evan told her. Then he told her about the condition of the cottages and the unpaid retirees. She was not surprised. Then he brought up the subject of Julia and Maria. "I am very concerned about their futures," he said.

"They still have their dowries, of course."

"No, they don't. My uncle went through the funds that were supposed to be set aside for their dowries. They have been left with nothing."

"Damn Philip!" Lady Barbara exclaimed. She glared at Evan as if he were the one at fault. "How could he be so irresponsible?"

"I have no idea," Evan replied. "But he was, and now I'm stuck with the consequences. I'll deal with the debt somehow, but the most pressing need is to make some arrangement for my cousins. They cannot continue on as they are."

There was a brief, charged silence. Then Lady Barbara said, "You have met Julia, of course."

"Yes."

"After Philip died, I offered to bring her and Maria here to Mereton, and she refused to come. She is as stubborn as a mule, that girl."

"I've noticed," Evan said with a flicker of humor. "Nevertheless, I am responsible for her and plans must be made for her future. I've been advised that my best course of action is to give her what Flora calls a 'season' so she can meet some eligible men and find a husband. I've also been told that you are giving a season to your own daughter, Aunt, and I have come to ask you to chaperone Julia as well."

Lady Barbara stared at him as if he was mad. "A London Season costs a fortune. I can't possibly undertake to sponsor her as well as Lizzie."

"I'll pay all of Julia's expenses. And I'll engage to give her a dowry as well. I'm going to have to mortgage Stoverton to raise cash and few thousand more pounds won't make much difference."

The expression on Lady Barbara's face hadn't changed. "Will Julia agree to go to London for the season?"

"I don't plan to give her a choice in the matter."

"You don't understand," Lady Barbara said, her hands fluttering in agitation. "If we drag Julia to London against her will, she will ruin everything for Lizzie. Do you know what she told me when I went to collect her and Maria to bring them here after Helen died?"

"No." Evan waited with real curiosity for her reply.

"She told me that if I forced her to come to my home she would make my life miserable. 'You don't want me in your house, Aunt Barbara, if I don't want to be there.' That's what she said, Evan! And the look on her face—she meant it. She's ruthless, Evan. I can't take a chance with my daughter's future."

Evan felt an unwilling surge of admiration for Julia. He said, "What if I can convince her to cooperate willingly with this Season business? Would you take her then?"

Just then the door opened, and a young girl came in. "Grantly told me that my cousin is here, Mama, and I have come to be introduced."

Evan stood and turned to face this new cousin. She was another Marshall, and a beautiful one. Her hair was more gold than silver and her eyes a lighter blue than his, but she could have been his sister, they looked so alike. "I'm your cousin Lizzie, my lord," she said, crossing to him and holding out her hand.

Evan took her hand into his. "I am delighted to meet you," he said. "And please, call me Evan."

Her smile was dazzling.

"Sit down, Lizzie," Lady Barbara said briskly. "What your cousin and I are discussing concerns you too. He wants me to bring out Julia along with you this Season."

Evan watched closely but no expression of alarm crossed Lizzie's classically beautiful face. "That seems sensible," she said sunnily as she took one of the crimson velvet chairs.

"I am afraid that Julia might not wish to join us," Lady Barbara said ominously.

Evan said, "Your mother is afraid that Julia might sabotage your own season if she is forced to do something she doesn't want to do."

Lizzie looked puzzled. "How could she do such a thing?"

"I can think of a whole list of things she could do if she chose to," Lady Barbara said grimly.

"But why wouldn't she want a season?" Lizzie asked. "How does she expect to find someone to wed if she doesn't go to London?"

"Don't ask me how Julia's mind works," Lady Barbara snapped. "It's unfathomable to me."

Evan brought up the offer Flora had recommended. "If you agree, Aunt, I should be pleased if you used the Piccadilly mansion as your base. I understand it's large and well-located."

Lady Barbara's expression changed. "Indeed. It is the perfect house from which to launch a young girl's come-out. The ballroom is fabulous."

Encouraged by this comment, Evan said, "If I can get Julia to promise to behave herself and cooperate with you, will you include her in Lizzie's season?"

Silence.

Lizzie said, "You have to, Mama. Julia has no mother or father. We have to help her."

Lovely and kind, Evan thought approvingly as he looked at Lizzie.

"All right," Lady Barbara said. "But I must speak to Julia herself to make certain she understands the standards I will expect her to uphold."

"Certainly," Evan said. "Don't worry, Aunt Barbara, I'll make everything clear to her."

During the two-hour drive home in the curricle, Evan thought about nothing except how he was going to present this idea to Julia and convince her to accept it.

Chapter Ten

After Evan left to pay a duty visit to Aunt Barbara, I saddled up Isabella and went to visit my dear friend, Sir Matthew Clarkson, our local squire. He was in one of the stalls with a pregnant mare, stroking her neck and murmuring to her soothingly.

"How's she doing?" I asked.

He turned to me. "She was a wee bit restless, but I think I've settled her down."

He gave the mare one last pat then joined me in the aisle. "I hear that the new earl has arrived from America."

I laughed. "Gossip in the village always runs like wildfire."

"What do you make of him?" Sir Matthew asked, raising his bushy white eyebrows.

"I'm not sure," I replied.

"Come along to the office and we'll have a chat."

We moved down the aisle to the comfortable old office, a small room where Sir Matthew kept a wide assortment of remedies for his horses and hounds' various ailments. There was a battered old desk in the corner with two chairs that were swathed in dark blue horse rugs. Once we were seated, Sir Matthew asked, "What does the new earl make of the financial disaster he inherited?"

"Mr. Shields recommended that he take a mortgage out on Stoverton." I scowled. "I hate the thought of it. It's like selling Stoverton to a bank."

Sir Matthew leaned back in his chair. "It's his only option, other than selling off the land, lass. And I know you'd hate that even more."

"I would," I said gloomily. "What I'd like best would be if he'd use his own money to bring Stoverton back to what it once was. He has millions of dollars, Sir Matthew! But that's not going to happen. He tells me he only makes investments that are going to earn him money." I glared. "The man looks exactly like the first earl, but he's a cit at heart!"

Sir Matthew said, "It would be grand if he'd spend his millions on Stoverton, but it's asking a lot of a stranger from another country. He feels none of the blood ties to Stoverton that you do. And a mortgage won't be so bad. If he makes regular payments, Stoverton will be free and clear once the mortgage is repaid. If he's as rich as you say he is, he should be able to do that easily enough."

I thought about that for a minute. Perhaps Sir Matthew was right. Perhaps a mortgage wouldn't be so bad after all. And if I was managing the property, I would make certain that every penny was put to good use. I could have Stoverton paying its own mortgage in a few years.

Sir Matthew cleared his throat. "Er...has the earl come up with any suggestions about your future, lass?"

I sat up straighter. "As a matter of fact, I have come up with a solution, Sir Matthew. I suggested to Evan that I could act as his agent here when he went back to America."

I bounced a little on the chair in my enthusiasm. "It's the perfect answer to both our problems. He doesn't want to remain in England, and I don't want to leave Stoverton. If he appoints me as his agent, then he can go home with the confidence that he has entrusted Stoverton to the best person possible."

There was a strange look on Sir Matthew's face. "Did you mention this idea to his lordship?"

"I did."

"And what did he say?"

"He said he'd think about it."

Sir Matthew closed his eyes and heaved a sigh. He opened his eyes and looked at me. "It's impossible, lass. If his lordship doesn't know it now, he soon will. You cannot be the agent for Stoverton."

I stared at him in astonishment. "Why not? No one knows more about the house and property than I do. I'm the perfect person for the job."

"You cannot do it, lass, because you're eighteen years old and the daughter of an earl. You're not a child any more, you're a young lady. The life you've been living cannot continue. You must marry a man of your own class and have your own home and family."

I stared at him in horror. "But I don't want to get married. If I got married I would have to move away from Stoverton."

Sir Matthew leaned toward me. "Julia." He never called me Julia. "You know I care for you. You're the daughter I never had. But you cannot give all your love to a building!"

To my horror I felt tears sting my eyes. "You really want me to go away? You wouldn't miss me?"

"I would miss you terribly. I meant it when I said I love you like a daughter. But all fathers have to let their daughters go eventually. It wouldn't be a sign of love if I tried to hang onto you. It would be selfishness. I have to recommend what I think is best for you, and I think the best thing would be to find a man you like and marry him."

I swallowed. "I see."

"Think about what I've said, lass. I know it isn't what you want to hear, but it's advice that comes from my heart."

I managed a shadowy smile, stood up and said, "I think I had better be getting along home now."

He nodded slowly and watched as I tried not to run out of the office.

*

What Sir Matthew said upset me profoundly. It wasn't that I didn't know that girls were expected to marry. It was just that I had never thought that expectation would apply to me. My mother had rarely taken me with her when she made calls on our neighbors, or attended the few local gatherings she deigned worthy of her presence. I had always thought it was because she was ashamed of me, but I didn't know what I could do to make her like me.

In the past, when I thought about my future, I assumed that my brother Philip would marry, and I would stay on at Stoverton while he and his wife lived mostly in London. I knew Philip would be perfectly happy to have me take care of his house and property. I wouldn't even have minded being a substitute parent to his children, as long as I could remain here, on this land that had belonged to my family for all these centuries.

You can't live all alone in this huge house, Evan had said.

I took Isabella to the stable and wouldn't let Toby unsaddle or groom her. I dawdled for as long as I could, putting some oil on her hooves so they wouldn't dry out and brushing her tail until Toby told me it would start to fall out if I didn't stop.

As I made my way to the house, I realized what the unfamiliar feeling in my chest was. Fear. My life wasn't in my own hands anymore, it was in the hands of this American, who had inherited land and a title he neither understood nor respected.

Stoverton was my land. I was the one who would love it and cherish it and keep alive the tradition of one of the greatest families in the history of England.

It was almost time for dinner when I reached the house and I went upstairs to my bedroom to put on one of the five dresses that hung in my wardrobe. There was a tall mirror in the corner of the room and, as always, I automatically went to check that my appearance was neat.

This time I stood and really looked at myself. For dinner I usually wore my long black hair knotted at the back of my head, an easy style for me to do by myself. My light gray eyes looked out from beneath my black brows and lashes, and the shabby blue dress, which had belonged to Maria when she was my size, was rather sad looking.

I knew I didn't live the life expected of an earl's daughter, but I lived the life I loved. And I was prepared to fight to keep it.

*

Cousin Flora dominated the dinner conversation, asking Evan about Lady Barbara and her plans. I didn't pay much attention; I was too busy trying to figure out how I could maneuver Evan into doing what I wanted him to do. Unfortunately, he did not appear to be a man easily manipulated.

I would come up with something, I thought. I had to.

After the pudding had been served, Evan asked if Flora would mind if I remained in the dining room with him so we could speak in private.

"Of course not," Flora said, much too effusively. "Come along, Maria. You can play the piano for me while your sister speaks to Evan."

Maria threw me an alarmed look. I kept my face blank and gestured for her to leave.

After the door had closed behind them, Evan picked up his glass of wine and came to sit across from me.

"You and I have to talk, Julia," he said. He proceeded to tell me about his visit to Aunt Barbara and her agreement to take me to London and present me along with Lizzie. I grew colder with every word he spoke.

"I don't want to go to London for a Season," I said. "I want to stay here."

He regarded me thoughtfully. "I've been thinking about your idea to take charge for me here at Stoverton, and I believe it has some merit," he said.

I lit up inside. "You do? That's wonderful, Evan! That's just...wonderful! I'll do a good job for you. I'll do the best job anyone could do."

"I know you would," he said. "But after meeting Aunt Barbara, and speaking to Flora, my original feeling has been confirmed. You can't be left here by yourself. Your family, the society you live in, won't allow it. And Maria needs you. You're all she has, and living alone here at Stoverton is not good for her."

He was speaking quietly and reasonably. And what he said about Maria was true. I bit my lip. "What do you think I should do?"

"You need to find a husband," he said.

"No! You want me to go and live in a strange place with some strange man? I can't do that, Evan!" I leaned toward him, desperate. "I can't!"

He didn't say what I expected to hear, that other girls did it all the time, why couldn't I? Instead he said, "We might be able to keep you at Stoverton, Julia."

I just stared.

"Think," he said. "You must marry. There's no getting around that. But you don't have to marry a man who has his own property. What if you picked a younger son, someone who would be happy to have a great estate he could live on?"

My mouth fell open.

"When we get to London, look around," he said. "You might find a man who likes all the things you like – horses and hunting, that sort of thing. You could continue to live at Stoverton and maybe you could even come to love him."

I doubted that, but the rest of his idea was worth thinking about.

"What about money? When a woman marries, her money becomes her husband's."

"The only money you will have, Julia, is my money, and your husband will have no right to that."

"But when I get Stoverton profitable again? We can't have the same thing happen that happened with Papa."

"Julia, your husband won't own Stoverton because it doesn't belong to you. He won't handle any of Stoverton's money. You will because I will designate you to be my agent."

He was right. It was a brilliant plan.

I said slowly, "So all I have to do is go to London with Aunt Barbara, go to all the boring parties she drags me to, and try to find a poverty-stricken husband who'll marry me for my dowry. And once I do that, I can come back to Stoverton to live?"

"Yes."

I smiled as I hadn't smiled since my father died. "Oh Evan, thank you!"

He blinked. Then he said, "It's a good business proposition for me as well. You're right when you say you know more about Stoverton than anyone else. The fact that you're a woman shouldn't stop you from using that knowledge, or me from taking advantage of it. My sister has run a multimillion-dollar business for years. And has borne two children, as well. I think you're the person for the job."

I bit my lip as an uncomfortable thought hit me. "But what if no one wants to marry me—even with the dowry? What will happen then?"

He favored me with that heart-catching smile. "You're a beautiful girl, Julia. Believe me, you'll have no problem finding a husband." His eyes narrowed to dangerous blue slits. "But you must follow Aunt Barbara's advice and be pleasant and accommodating to her and to your cousin. I must also tell you that Aunt Barbara has agreed to include Maria in her household and find her a proper governess and a good music teacher."

I thought about having to listen to Aunt Barbara and repressed a shudder. *I can do it,* I told myself. I have to do it. The prize would be Stoverton, and Stoverton was worth any sacrifice.

I managed to say, "I will do whatever Aunt Barbara tells me to."

He blessed me with the smile again. "Good girl. I'll send word to Aunt Barbara tomorrow that all has been agreed to. She plans to leave for London in a week."

"A week! That's not much notice!"

"It's not as if you have a lot to pack," he said dryly.

"Yes, but I have to make sure the hay is ordered and the...."

He cut me off. "I will leave enough money with Toby for him to manage. You trust him, don't you?"

"Yes."

He stood up. "Good. Then let's go into the library and tell the good news to Flora and Maria."

I stood as well. I felt as if my head was whirling. "All right," I said, and allowed him to take my elbow and steer me out of the room.

Chapter Eleven

Evan was jerked out of sleep by the sound of screaming. He leaped out of bed, ran out into the hall in his nightshirt and saw Maria opening the door to Julia's bedroom. Without thinking, he raced down the hall and followed her inside.

The window in Julia's room was uncovered and the moonlight shone directly in, giving Evan a clear look at the picture in front of him. Julia was sitting with her face in her hands and Maria had her arms around her sister's shoulders. Julia's breathing was audible—harsh, fast and frightened.

He walked slowly toward the bed and said, as quietly and calmly as he could, "What has happened?"

Julia's head jerked up when she heard his voice. "Nothing! Just a silly dream. I'm sorry I disturbed everyone. Go back to bed. I'll be fine."

Her long silky black hair was tumbling around her shoulders and she was as pale as the sheets on her bed. Her gray eyes were dark with terror. He wanted to sit on the bed beside her and take her into his arms. He wanted to stroke that beautiful hair and murmur that she was safe with him, that he would never let anything bad happen to her.

Maria said, "I'll stay with her, Evan. Go back to bed."

His head went up, as if someone had slapped him. He looked at the two girls and realized Maria was right; he should leave. He backed away murmuring something about being on call if he was needed. He closed the door behind him as he stepped into the hall.

Back in his own room he had trouble falling asleep. What kind of nightmare could have reduced Julia to such terror? As for his own reaction…he would have felt exactly the same if it had been Maria who had waked from a nightmare. He told himself this so forcefully that he almost believed it.

*

Julia was not at breakfast the following morning. When Flora asked after her, Maria said she was at the stable, going over last-minute things with Toby.

Flora looked annoyed. "Lady Barbara will arrive this afternoon. I hope Julia is going to be here, properly dressed, when she gets here."

Apparently Flora had slept through Julia's nightmare. Evan said, "Of course she'll be here. She has promised to be courteous to my aunt and I don't think Julia is one to go back on her promises."

Maria gave him a grateful smile. "No, she isn't."

When breakfast was over, Evan said, "Maria, may I speak to you for a moment?"

Maria looked at Flora, who said, "Don't keep her, Evan."

"I won't."

Once the door closed behind Flora, Evan sat at the table and gestured Maria to the chair beside him. "What happened last night?"

"Julia had the dream about Papa. It doesn't happen often, but it upsets her when it does."

"A dream about your father?"

Maria looked at him more closely. "Julia was the one who found Papa's body. He'd shot himself in the head. Didn't you know that?"

Evan felt as if he had just received an unexpected punch in the stomach. "No, I didn't. What a dreadful experience!"

"She's never described it to me, but I heard the magistrate talking to his men. It sounded horrid; I can't imagine what it must have felt like to see it."

"Poor, brave little Julia," Evan said softly. He shook his head in disgust. "My uncle left her to find his body. What a miserable creature he must have been."

"Don't ever mention to Julia I told you this," Maria warned. "In fact, don't ever mention that you saw her last night. She hates being weak."

"It's not weak to have a nightmare when you've seen a nightmare," Evan protested.

"Julia doesn't think like that."

Evan sighed. "No, I suppose she doesn't. Well, we must hope that with the passing of time the nightmares will fade."

Maria nodded. "Yes."

"Maria!" It was Flora at the door. "I want you to pick out the music you want to take."

Maria shot Evan an apologetic smile and went to join Flora.

*

Lady Barbara and Elizabeth arrived halfway through the afternoon. Evan was walking toward the house when he saw the coach arrive, so he was the first to welcome his aunt and cousin to Stoverton. Aside from the mountain of luggage that accompanied her in a second coach, Lady Barbara informed him she was bringing to London two personal maids, her coachman, and a groom. She had already sent her butler on ahead to hire household staff.

Evan received this news without changing expression and escorted his aunt and cousin to the drawing room, where Flora sat sewing by the light coming in through one of the tall windows. She invited Lady Barbara and Lizzie to sit on two matching tapestry chairs nearby and Evan joined them.

Lizzie looked up at the picture of the first earl in his Elizabethan finery. "It's amazing how much you look like him, Cousin Evan," she said.

"It is amazing," Lady Barbara agreed. "The Marshalls have always been blue-eyed and fair-haired, but none of us ever looked so like a replica of Philip."

Lucy came in with the tea tray and Flora poured. Once everyone had a cup, she asked Lady Barbara how her journey had been.

"I should hardly call a two-hour trip a journey, Flora," Lady Barbara replied. She turned her attention to Evan. "I never asked. Is Flora to come with us?"

Evan wondered if his aunt was being deliberately rude or if she just didn't know any better. "I believe Flora is able to speak for herself, Aunt," he replied.

"I am going to my sister's home," Flora said quietly. "Evan is going to hire a governess for Maria, so she won't need me, and my sister has been recently widowed and desires my company."

"Good," Lady Barbara said.

Evan said deliberately, "We'll miss you, Cousin Flora. You did the girls a great service by coming here, and your company has been a pleasure to all of us."

She gave him a grateful smile.

The door opened and Maria came in. She went to kiss her aunt and get a hug from Lizzie.

"Good heavens, child!" Lady Barbara said, watching Maria as she moved toward Evan. "That dress is much too small for you. Don't you have anything better?"

Evan wondered if all great English ladies were rude. He said, "I would like it if you would buy new clothes for Maria as well as Julia when you get to London, Aunt."

"Oh yes!" Lizzie bestowed a dazzling smile on Maria. "Just think how much fun it's going to be! All that shopping!"

Maria's face lit with an answering smile. Evan looked at Lizzie with pleasure. What a nice girl she was.

Flora asked Lady Barbara, "Will Mr. Lewis be going to London with you?"

"He'll put in an appearance for the come-out ball, of course, but his duties as local magistrate keep him busy at home." She turned to her nephew. "And since we'll have Evan for an escort, we won't need him."

Evan put his cup down on the table beside him and directed an amazed blue stare at his aunt. "What precisely do you mean by my 'services as an escort,' Aunt? I am accompanying you to London because I have business there. I have no plans to socialize with a crowd of English aristocrats."

"But you must, Evan!" Lizzie's lighter blue eyes regarded him imploringly. "We need a gentleman escort if we're to go to balls. You don't have to come to everything we do, but you have to come with us to dances. And to Almacks."

Evan shook his head. "I'm afraid you must get your father for this detail, Lizzie. I have other things to attend to."

Lady Barbara opened her mouth to speak, but before any words came out, the door opened once again and Julia was there. She stood for a moment, regarding her relatives seated by the window. She wore her old riding skirt and boots; her red jacket was open showing a plain white blouse tucked in at the waist. Her ebony hair was tied at her nape and spilled down between her shoulders halfway to her waist.

She didn't say a word, but everyone in the room immediately turned to look at her.

Evan knew it was possible to dominate a room by sheer personal magnetism. He did it himself all the time. But he was a very large man. It was interesting that this small, black-haired girl had the same power.

"Hullo," Julia said. "I got your horses settled down, Aunt Barbara."

"I brought a groom to do that," Lady Barbara replied tersely.

"I showed the groom where he could sleep as well."

Lady Barbara's nose seemed to pinch together. When she spoke, her voice sounded carefully composed. "Come and give me a kiss, Julia."

Unflinchingly, Julia marched across the floor and bestowed a quick salute on her aunt's cheek. She turned to her cousin. "How are you, Lizzie?"

Lizzie beamed back. "I'm so happy you are going to make your come-out with me, Julia! We'll have such fun!"

Julia twitched her lips in what Evan assumed was supposed to be a smile.

Flora said, "You two will be the most beautiful girls in London—one so fair and one so dark. You'll be the belles of the season."

Lizzie trilled light laughter and Julia quirked her lips.

She's trying, Evan told himself resolutely.

Lady Barbara said, "Is that the ensemble you greet guests in?"

"It's my favorite 'ensemble'" Julia replied. "I don't have much else."

Lady Barbara turned her blue gaze to Evan. "Appropriate wardrobes will be very expensive. Be prepared."

Evan waved a hand indicating largesse. "Whatever it takes."

Julia said, "There's no reason for Evan to spend a lot of money. I can call in Mrs. Wrentham from the village. She's often made our clothes and she's quite reasonable."

Lady Barbara looked aghast. "No one from the village is going to make your clothes, Julia! We will remove to London immediately and visit the best modistes on Bond Street. It's unfortunate that you're so small, but your figure is slender. I think we'll be able to dress you very well."

Julia's gray eyes were getting darker—not a good sign.

"We'll certainly have to get you a new riding habit!" Lady Barbara added, looking at Julia's present costume.

For the first time, Julia looked interested. "Where does one ride in London?" she asked her aunt.

"Hyde Park," Lady Barbara replied immediately. "At five o'clock in the afternoon you can see the whole world in Hyde Park."

Julia looked at Evan. "I'll need to bring Isabella."

"Of course," Evan said. He was feeling a little guilty about saddling her with Lady Barbara, so he said, "If you don't want to take Isabella away from the country, we could buy you another horse for London. You're always saying there aren't enough horses at Stoverton. I'm sure we can afford to add one more."

Her lips parted slightly. Her wonderful eyes enlarged. "Do you mean that?"

"Yes."

"Tattersalls is the place to look for horses in London." A note of excitement rang in her voice. "We could go there. I've always wanted to see Tattersalls."

"A lady never goes to Tattersalls," Lady Barbara said ominously. "You would be utterly disgraced should you ever do such a thing. And a horse is the least of our needs at the moment, Julia! We first must concentrate on your wardrobe."

Julia said pleasantly, "If I can't ride I will be unhappy, Aunt Barbara. And when I'm unhappy I'm not very nice to be around."

Evan pretended to cough to hide his amusement.

Lady Barbara was glaring at him. He said hastily, "We'll get you a horse, Julia. I promise. Do you remember *your* promise?"

He saw her breast rise and fall as she drew a deep breath. "Yes," she said baldly. And went to sit next to Maria.

*

Lady Barbara wished to be on the road to London as quickly as possible. "We have so much to do before the Season starts! There are wardrobes to purchase and heaven knows what state Philip has left Althorpe house in. My butler has had only a week to restore it to some kind of order."

While Lady Barbara supervised what little clothing Maria and Julia were to take, Evan spent his time looking at the older account books for the estate, trying to figure out how expensive Stoverton would be to run when it wasn't encumbered by debt.

The afternoon before they were due to depart, Evan was in the library when Julia sought him out. "You weren't just trying to placate me when you said you'd buy me a horse, were you Evan?"

He looked up from his book. "Julia, I don't know what kind of people you are accustomed to dealing with, but in America a man's word is as good as his bond. If I say I am going to do something, I will do it. Do you understand me?"

"Yes," she said. "Sorry."

She took a step back as if she was going to leave, when he asked, "Have you ever been to London?"

"I might have gone sometime when I was a child, but I have no memory of it."

He said, "I made a brief stop in the city before I came out to Stoverton, but I didn't get a chance to look around." He gestured to the book in front of him. "Look. It's a guidebook of London I found on one of the shelves. If we're going to be in the city, we might as well take in the sights."

She came to stand at his shoulder. "I've always wanted to see Astley's Equestrian Circus. I used to ask to be taken for my birthday, but it never seemed to be convenient."

Evan looked down again at the book to hide his expression. It seemed to him that nothing about their children had ever been convenient to the earl and his wife.

He flipped a page. "Here, I think this is Astley's." She bent to look at the picture of a white horse balanced in a perfect rear and her breast brushed against his shoulder.

"Isn't that amazing?" She seemed completely unaware of how close they were. "It's very difficult for a horse to do that you know."

He could smell the scent of her hair. What was it, he wondered? Lavender?

"We'll have to go and see it," he said, his voice a little huskier than usual.

She turned her head toward him and smiled. His breath caught. Her eyelashes were so long and black they made her gray eyes even more remarkable. "That would be wonderful!"

She straightened up and his brain began to work again. She said, "Perhaps they'll be a balloon ascension while we're there. Maria would like that."

"I would like that too," he said, pleased to hear that his voice sounded normal.

"You'll like Astley's too," she promised.

He waved his hand at a chair placed at a safe distance. "Sit for a minute."

She sat.

He said, "I'm sick to death of Aunt Barbara pestering me about escorting you girls to dances! Do you think you can convince her to just send for her husband and leave me alone?"

"I hate dances and I have to go. Why shouldn't you?"

"You've never been to a dance. How do you know you'll hate it?"

"It's not the dancing. It's because I don't like talking a lot of nonsense to people I don't know. Why don't *you* want to go?"

"Because I don't like the English aristocracy. When we signed our declaration of independence from Britain, do you know what we declared to be the foundation on which the United States was to be built?"

"No. Nor do I care."

He ignored the latter part of her comment. "This is what Mr. Jefferson wrote, and what all thirteen colonies signed: *We hold these truths to be self-evident, that all men are created equal, that they are endowed by their Creator with certain unalienable Rights, that among these are Life, Liberty and the pursuit of Happiness. "*

He looked into her eyes. "That is what my country is about, Julia. We do not have, nor will we ever have, an hereditary aristocracy. In America all men are equal."

"It sounds noble," she said. "But so did the French sound noble when they started their revolution, and look how that ended. Do you really think you can do it?"

"We are doing it. We're new and we're learning, but we have vast tracts of land open in our west and opportunities for every person who wants to take advantage of them. Look at my father. He didn't make his money because he was a Marshall. He made his money because he was smart enough to create his own business and do a damn good job of running it."

She shook her head and a strand of silky black hair came loose from its tie and fell across her cheek. "But don't you see? One of the reasons he was such an extraordinary man was because Marshall blood ran in his veins. I think you should come to some social events in London. It would be good for you learn to appreciate your English heritage. You may be an American, but in your blood and your bones you are a Marshall. Your ancestors are inextricably bound up with the history of this country."

She leaned toward him in her eagerness to make him understand. "Marshall blood has bled for England in every war she ever fought. One Marshall was even a Prime Minister. You may not choose to embrace England as your home, but you should *know* these things, Evan. In my father you have seen the worst of the family. Get to know the best."

He leaned away from her. "I have never belittled the importance of family. I was very close to my parents; I am still very close to my sister. But that's where my family is, Julia, in America. Not here."

"Your family is in both places," she replied.

He changed the subject by regarding her worn riding skirt. "I'm looking forward to seeing you in a pretty dress for a change."

"Aunt Barbara didn't seem to think much of your wardrobe either," she retorted.

He looked gloomy. "No. She didn't."

Her voice, usually so crisp and definite, took on a coaxing note. "Evan, if we face the ordeal of this season together, it might make it more bearable."

"For who?" he asked.

"For both of us. You can't skulk around London while we're trailing around to balls and breakfasts and musical evenings and whatever other horror Aunt Barbara has planned. It would look strange. Besides," her voice grew serious, "don't you think it's your duty to do what you can to smooth out the relations between our two countries?"

This from the girl who had told him she hated everything about America.

He said, "We have a Minister in London whose job it is to do just that. John Quincy Adams, the son of our second president. He's a brilliant man and will do just fine."

Evan said this with confidence, but in his heart he was not so sure about the powers of John Quincy Adams to deal with the British. The Minister was brilliant; no one would question that. But he was also an extremely difficult man, overbearing, dogmatic, rude, and strictly puritan in his moral code. Evan had met with the Minister several times when he first arrived in London and had been impressed by his intellect and appalled by his manners.

Julia said, "You are perfectly positioned to help Mr. Adams. You said you don't like the English. Well the English are not much in love with Americans either, Evan. That battle in New Orleans, which was fought *after* the treaty was signed, has made you a lot of enemies."

"How do you know that?"

"Sir Matthew Clarkson, our local squire, told me about it. He gets the papers from London."

"I don't think I've met him."

"He's the local Master of Fox Hounds. I hunt with his pack. He's a great friend of mine."

This must be the man Lady Barbara had so deplored.

Julia said, "I must remember to see if I can find some medicine for his lumbago while I'm in London. He almost had to miss the last two hunts because his back was acting up so badly."

Evan said, "It's probably not a bad idea for me to keep an eye on your prospective suitors." He owed it to Julia to make sure she married a decent man, he told himself. She had no one else to look out for her interests. She had tilted her head in a way that showed off her long lovely neck. He looked away hastily and said, "I don't want you to fall in love with one of the riders at Astley's equestrian circus."

"That will never happen. I might fall in love with his horse, though."

She laughed at the expression on his face and, after a moment, he began to laugh too.

Chapter Twelve

We left for London on a windy morning in late March. Maria, Flora and I rode in my father's coach, which was pulled by our four old carriage horses. Although London wasn't a great distance from Stoverton, I insisted that our driver, who was Toby's nephew, stop several times along the way to rest the poor animals. They hadn't had this much exercise in years.

Althorpe House had been the family's London residence for a hundred years and I was curious to see it. I had read about it in one of the books in our library and learned it was quite famous. It had been designed by the famous architect Colen Campbell and decorated by the Venetian artists Giacomo Pellerini and Sebastiano Ricci. It was supposed to be one of the grandest houses in London, which was why my mother had spent so much of her time there, reigning over the *ton*.

When the carriage swung through the elaborate iron gate and into the courtyard, I popped my head out one window and Maria popped hers out the other. My mouth dropped open as I looked around. The courtyard was framed on either side by two graceful, colonnaded buildings. In the center of these buildings was a large Palladian style house, with eleven bays, projecting slightly at either end and in the center. I had seen pictures of typical London town houses; this was not remotely like the narrow, closely crowded buildings where most of the *ton* lived while they were in London.

While Maria and I were still gaping, a footman came running down the front stairs followed more slowly by Evan, who had ridden Baron and so arrived before us. He came to open the coach door and, before the footman could set the steps, he reached up, put his hands around my waist and lifted me down. Then he did the same thing for Maria.

His big hands had almost fit around my waist; for some reason this made me feel peculiar. I blinked twice, shook my head, and turned to stare at the house.

"My goodness," Maria said. "It's big."

"It's a bloody palace," Evan growled.

I knew what he was thinking. It was going to cost him a fortune to run this place.

Maria said tentatively, "Don't let Aunt Barbara hear you say that word, Evan. She'll yell at you."

Evan looked penitent. "I'm sorry, Maria. I shouldn't swear in front of you."

"Oh it doesn't bother me. Julia swears all the time," Maria assured him blithely. "But Aunt Barbara won't like it."

The butler, whom my aunt had sent on ahead, was waiting for us in the doorway. We went inside and found Aunt Barbara standing in the hall.

"What took you so long?" she demanded. "We've been here for almost an hour."

"We stopped a few times to rest the horses. They're old and haven't made a journey like this in years."

"I have been waiting for you to arrive to give Evan a tour of the house. Had I known it would take you so long I would not have been so thoughtful."

I really wanted to see the house so I gave her an apologetic smile and said I was sorry we had kept her waiting.

"Oh good, you're here." It was Lizzie, coming down the hall. "Isn't this place amazing?"

"It certainly is." Evan's voice was carefully neutral. I shot him a look. He was the one who had dragged me here, I thought, and if it cost him a small fortune, it wasn't my fault.

We were standing in the entrance hall, which was a grand affair with columns that reminded me of a Greek temple. The floor was paved in marble. My aunt gathered us up and ushered us into the first room off the hall, which was a small drawing room, used I supposed, for callers to wait to see if they would be admitted by the occupants. It had several wonderful landscape paintings on its walls.

After we looked at the drawing room, Aunt Barbara ushered us back into the hallway, which was paved with the same marble as the entrance hall. It was also lined with busts of Roman and Greek gods and heroes displayed on marble pedestals. All of the main rooms opened off this hallway and Aunt Barbara took us into each one of them.

We saw a music room, which held a harpsichord, a harp and a piano. I was thrilled to see the piano for Maria's sake. We saw a huge drawing room, with a beautifully sculptured ceiling and frescos painted on the walls. The dining room could easily seat forty people and had an enormous crystal chandelier that sparkled with cleanliness. The library was a vast room, with floor to ceiling windows. The shelves that lined the room were all enclosed in glass and the carpet was from Turkey and must have cost a fortune. The remaining rooms on this floor were the earl and countess's sleeping quarters and dressing rooms, which we didn't go into.

Two gracefully curved staircases rose to the next floor, at the top of which was an immense ballroom. Lady Barbara pointed this out with great satisfaction. "This is where we will have Lizzie's...and Julia's...come-out ball. It is the finest ballroom in London."

As we followed my aunt through the house, the thing that most excited me wasn't the size of the rooms or the splendor of the furnishings; it was the paintings. I had known my grandfather was a great collector of art, but I had always thought all of the valuable pieces were at Stoverton. Not so.

Hanging on the walls of Althorpe House were two Veroneses, a Giordano, several Tintorettos and Titians, a Vermeer and two lush portraits by Rubens. There were also several landscapes by Constable, an artist Aunt Barbara told us her father had liked very much.

Evan's comment was typical. "I suppose these pictures are valuable."

"Very valuable," Aunt Barbara returned. "This house is included in the entail or my brother would surely have sold them all."

Evan was looking thoughtful. "This house is a more recent acquisition than Stoverton, right? I mean, it doesn't have the same historical value."

"No. But it cost a fortune to build and furnish," Aunt Barbara said.

"Can entails ever be changed?" Evan asked next.

Aha, I thought. He's thinking he might be able to sell this house.

"I don't think so," Aunt Barbara replied. "What are you thinking of doing? Selling it to some rich cit?" She looked as if she had just smelled some noxious odor.

"Cit?" Evan said. "What's a cit?"

"A cit is a person of the middle-class who has made his money in manufacture or some other such sordid endeavor."

Evan said mildly, "Well, I guess that makes me a cit, then."

"Don't be ridiculous. Your father was the son of an earl. Of course you're not a cit!"

"My mother was the daughter of a housekeeper," Evan returned, still speaking mildly.

"No one will hold that against you," Lady Barbara assured him. "One has only to look at you to know you're a Marshall. And you hold one of the oldest titles in the country." She patted his arm. "Don't worry. You will be embraced by polite society."

I didn't think Evan had been at all worried about what English polite society thought of him. He saw me looking at him and winked. I had to look down to smother a smile.

The other public rooms on the ballroom floor were less formal than the rest of the house. The furniture looked more comfortable and in one there was a table by the window with a chess set laid out upon it. A picture of Stoverton hung over the mantle and in the far corner of the room, next to a curio cabinet, was a suit of medieval armor.

Evan strode over to the armor and began to examine it curiously. I went to join him.

"How could those fellows bear to enclose themselves in this contraption?" he asked as he lifted the facemask. "It doesn't seem as if one would be able to move at all. Or breathe."

"It certainly doesn't look very comfortable," I agreed. I turned my head. "Did this armor belong to someone in the family, Aunt Barbara?"

My aunt crossed the floor to stand beside us. "Yes. It is supposed to have belonged to the first Philip Marshall; he wore it at Crecy." She swiped her finger along the mailed glove and wrinkled her nose in disgust. "I don't believe this has been dusted since Helen died. I shall tell Grantly to get one of the maids to clean it up. We cannot have this kind of slovenliness if we are to reside here."

Evan was still looking at the armor. "This fellow appeared to be pretty tall. I thought men in those days were short."

"Marshalls have always been tall." Aunt Barbara informed him.

"Except for Julia," Lizzie said cheerfully, coming up to join us. "She's so small and delicate looking. I feel like a great gawky creature with too many hands and feet when I stand next to her."

Delicate? I stared at her in outrage. One thing I am not is delicate. I opened my mouth to snap at Lizzie and felt a hand close around my forearm.

It was Evan. He squeezed, then let me go. I closed my mouth and swallowed my words. "I look like my mother's side of the family," I muttered.

I caught Aunt Barbara looking at me with a strange expression in her eyes, but before I could ask her what she was thinking, the housekeeper joined us.

She curtseyed to Evan. "How do you do, my lord. I am Margaret Sales, your housekeeper. I am so sorry that I was not here to greet you. I was in the kitchen discussing menus with the cook."

I watched Evan give her his irresistible smile. "How do you do, Mrs. Sales. It's nice of you to help us out. I hope you have been made comfortable yourself."

The housekeeper looked a little surprised, but replied, "I am very comfortable, my lord, thank you."

"What rooms have you had made up?" Aunt Barbara said.

"The earl's chamber is ready for his lordship. And I have had the blue, yellow, rose and gold bedrooms made up for you and the young ladies," Mrs. Sales returned.

"We will have tea in here and give the servants a chance to bring up the luggage," Lady Barbara decreed.

Evan said, "Instead of tea, Mrs. Sales, I'll have a glass of ale if you have it."

"I'll have someone bring it to you, my lord."

"Thank you." Evan gestured to the sofas that were placed before the carved wood fireplace. "This is what I call a comfortable room. "Let's all sit down and Aunt Barbara can tell us what she has planned for us to do tomorrow."

Obediently we trooped to the sofas and made ourselves at home.

Chapter Thirteen

The following morning, Lady Barbara hustled Lizzie, Julia and Maria into her carriage to go shopping. Evan watched them go with amusement. Lizzie and Maria looked excited; Julia looked resigned.

After the ladies had left, he went into the library, sat behind the big mahogany desk, leaned back in the comfortable chair and clasped his hands behind his head.

This little excursion to London was going to cost him a fortune. The house was huge and everywhere he looked he saw a servant. He had managed to stop his aunt before she left on her shopping expedition to tell her that he would pay for Maria and Julia's clothes, but he was not treating Lizzie to a new wardrobe too.

Lady Barbara had gotten quite huffy. Of course Lizzie's father would pay for her clothing!

Evan had apologized if he had offended her, but he was a canny Yankee and he wouldn't have put it past his aunt to put Lizzie's clothes on his bill. He could tell she was already aiming to make him pay for this big fancy come-out party she kept going on about. He would have to disabuse her of that notion too. He was willing to go half with her, and to let her use his house, but he thought he was already shouldering more than his fair share of the burden of this damned season. She had hired a ton of servants and he was going to have to work like a Trojan to remember so many new names. Not to mention the fact that he was the one who had to pay their salaries.

He came back into an upright position and his eyes fell on the collection of small bible scenes that his aunt had said were done by a fellow named Rubens. He got up and went over to look at them closely.

They were very nice, he thought. He liked them. They suited this wood-paneled, book-lined room. But then, he had liked a number of the pictures that his aunt and Julia had dismissed as being 'worth nothing.' What made one landscape of trees and cows and a stream more 'valuable' than another?

I wish I knew more about art, he thought, as he returned to his chair. His father had grown up in this world, but he had never attempted to pass along to his children any of his cultural knowledge. They had had some pretty landscapes in the house on Chestnut Street, landscapes like the ones Julia had turned her nose up at. His father had always seemed to be perfectly happy with them.

Evan looked down at the desk, which had several drawers. He went through them methodically. Most of them contained dunning letters from merchants who had not been paid. Mr. Shields had said he would put the word out amongst all of his uncle's creditors that the new earl was intending to pay the overdue bills in full as soon as he could make proper arrangements with a bank. "That should give you at least a month before they start sending bailiffs to invade your house," the attorney had assured him.

Evan had stared with horror at Shields. "Invade my house?"

"Oh, yes. They'll move right in with you if you get too far behind. It's embarrassing."

"I should think so!" Evan had returned.

As he sat there frowning at the bills in front of him, a footman came in to tell him that he had a visitor. "Mr. Roger Spenser, my lord."

Evan smiled. "Thank you," he said to the young man who had delivered this message. "What is your name? There are so many new people for me to get to know that you will have to excuse me if I am a little slow to remember who everyone is."

The footman, a tall, dark-haired boy with a narrow chin, looked surprised by this statement. "I'm Sidney, my lord."

"Sidney. Good. Well, thank you Sidney. You may bring Mr. Spenser to me here in the library."

As soon as a stocky gray-haired man dressed correctly in a blue morning coat and beige pantaloons came in the door, Evan jumped to his feet and went to greet him.

"Mr. Spenser! It is so kind of you to call. I was hoping to see you."

"My lord, how wonderful it is to meet your father's son." The older man squeezed Evan's hand hard. "You look very like him."

"I appear to look like a great many previous Marshalls," Evan said wryly. "But, please, don't call me 'my lord.' I am a good American and it grates on my republican sensibilities. Call me Evan." He gestured to the upholstered chairs that were placed before the fireplace where glowing coals were heating the room nicely. "Won't you come and sit down?"

The two men took seats facing each other. "May I offer you some refreshment?" Evan asked.

"Thank you, my boy, but no. What you can do is tell me how I may be of service to you. I know you have walked into a hornet's nest of debt. Everyone in London knows that, I am sorry to say. And you are a stranger here. If I can be of any help at all, please call on me."

"Thank you," Evan said, and brought up what had been on his mind ever since he first set foot in Althorpe House. "To be honest, Mr. Spenser, what I need more than anything else is an attorney who can break the entail on this house. Would you perhaps know of such a person?"

Spenser narrowed his eyes in thought. Then he said slowly, "I'll tell you what, my boy, go and see Joshua Rothschild. He's a relative of *the* Rothschilds and the cleverest cove I know. If there's any way to break that entail, he'll find it. He has his offices in the city – I'll write down the address for you before I leave."

Evan smiled gratefully. "Thank you, sir. Mr. Shields is a competent man, but I need someone who is more than just competent for this task."

"Go to see Rothschild."

"I will. Shall I give him your name as a reference?"

Spenser laughed. "Your reference is your title, Evan. No one will refuse to see the Earl of Althorpe, believe me."

Evan, who wholeheartedly disapproved of titles, was relieved to hear this Rothschild genius would see him because he had one. He was determined to at least break the part of the entail that related to the fortune in art that hung in this benighted house.

"I was so sorry to hear about the death of your father," Spenser said. "And at such a young age."

"I know." An old pain stabbed, sudden and sharp, in Evan's heart. *I wonder if I'll ever get over missing them,* he thought.

He said to his father's old friend, "Do you know my father never once told me that he was the son of an earl?"

Spenser gave a dry, raspy laugh. "How like Tommy. What did you think of Stoverton when you saw it?"

"I was stunned. And this house also—the both of them— they're huge."

"They are that," Spenser agreed. "I spent several school holidays at Stoverton with your father so I have seen the place. It was a wonderful spot for boys to play."

Evan leaned forward. "If you wouldn't mind, I would love to hear more about my father's boyhood."

"I'm not surprised that Tommy didn't dwell on his past very much. He was always a boy capable of tremendous focus. If he wanted something, he went after it with single-minded determination. He did that when he decided to marry your mother, and it appears he did it again when he decided to adopt America as his country."

"Yes," Evan agreed. "My father did have enormous focus. But I could wish that he had shared more about England with me. I feel very much like a fish out of water, I'm afraid."

Spenser returned reassuringly, "You'll do fine, my boy. And if you want to hear tales of your father's youth, you've come to the right place." Spenser settled back in his chair and folded his hands on his comfortable stomach. "Tommy and I met on the first day we both came to Eton…"

When Mr. Spenser had finished his stories, Evan asked him, "What do you think about Napoleon's leaving Elba and making it back to France? Will he be able to gather enough troops to force another battle?"

"We have to assume he will," Spenser replied. "Wellington is in Brussels now gathering our own troops, and the allies are doing the same. We have to be prepared if Napoleon comes after us."

Evan said ironically, "I find myself in a bit of a quandary. France has always been America's ally, you know. Her help was crucial in winning our independence. If the people of France prefer Napoleon to the return of that musty old Bourbon king you foisted upon them, I rather think they should be allowed to make that choice."

Spenser pulled thoughtfully on his chin. "Napoleon isn't another Washington, Evan," he said. "Don't forget, Napoleon made himself an emperor, not a president. He tried to enslave all of Europe. For the sake of world peace, he must be defeated."

Evan decided that this was not a topic they could explore with any semblance of detachment, so he once again changed the subject. "I do have one other favor to beg of you, Mr. Spenser."

"Certainly."

"My aunt informs me that she will not be seen with me in public unless I spruce up my wardrobe. Would you mind giving me your company to make sure I get rigged out with all the right stuff?"

Spenser laughed. "I would be happy to, my boy. I know just the tailor you should see."

"Thank you," Evan replied sincerely. "Now, won't you please have a glass of wine with me?"

Mr. Spenser smiled. "Well, perhaps I will. Perhaps I will."

Evan smiled back.

Chapter Fourteen

A day's shopping with Aunt Barbara was more exhausting than an all-day hunt. By early afternoon I thought I'd collapse if one more person pinned a dress around me. Aunt Barbara ordered carriage dresses, dinner dresses, evening dresses, morning dresses, promenade dresses, riding dresses, theatre dresses and walking dresses. I resolutely squashed my flare of sympathy for Evan, who would be stuck paying for all of this. After all, it was he who had insisted that I come to London.

The one thing that kept me going all day with a semblance of good grace was the evident delight Maria felt as she watched me trying on dress after dress.

"You look beautiful, Julia," she said, over and over again. It made me feel good to see her so happy.

Lizzie was surprisingly good company. She was so genuinely nice that it was impossible to dislike her. Disliking Lizzie would be like disliking a good-natured dog.

"I'm ravenous," Lizzie declared as the carriage finally pulled up before the front of Althorpe House.

I was too. I said to Lizzie, "Let's check the kitchen to see what we can scavenge."

Aunt Barbara frowned direfully. "A lady does not go to the kitchen, Julia. The proper etiquette is to ring for what you desire."

I bit my tongue and said nothing. When Aunt Barbara had gone upstairs the three of us left standing in the hall looked at each other. Lizzie said, "I'm sure no one will mind if we go to the kitchen." She smiled entrancingly. "Perhaps Cook will have some of that cake we had last night left."

Maria said, "Yum."

I grinned at my sister, then turned to Lizzie. "Let's do it."

Without another word the three of us trooped off to the kitchen.

*

After dinner, when we had retired to the upstairs drawing room, Aunt Barbara brought up the subject of dancing. "What sort of dances do you do in America?" she asked Evan.

He was leaning his shoulders up against the chestnut mantelpiece, looking so like the first earl's portrait that hung over the fireplace at home that he almost took my breath away.

This happened to me occasionally. I would look at him and get this strange feeling in my stomach, as if I had been wafted back in time and my Philip was standing right there in the room with me. I knew that Evan wasn't Philip, of course, but there was something about his presence that caused this peculiar flutter in my stomach.

When I brought my attention back to the conversation, Aunt Barbara was saying to him, "Country dances and cotillions are all very well, but do you know the quadrille and the waltz?"

"No," Evan said.

"So I thought." Aunt Barbara next turned to me. "What dances do *you* know, Julia?"

I knew the same country-dances as Evan; dances I had learned as a child. I had liked to dance when I was young. It was fun swishing around in time to the music.

"I don't know the quadrille or the waltz either," I said.

Lizzie said breathlessly, "Oh, Mama, are we really going to be allowed to waltz?"

"The waltz is going to be danced at Almack's this year, Lizzie.

"Is there something special about the waltz?" I asked.

"It was considered very risqué when it was first introduced here from Vienna, but the patronesses of Almack's have declared it acceptable this year so you and Lizzie must learn it," my aunt informed me.

Lizzie clapped her hands in delight.

"Why is this Almack's approval so important?" Evan asked.

I knew about Almack's because my mother had been one of the patronesses. I wasn't quite sure what kind of place it was, but I knew if my mother patronized it, it was important.

Lizzie answered Evan's question with a laugh. "It's called the 'marriage mart,' Evan.

"It's where a girl goes to find a husband."

"Elizabeth, you sound like a cit," Aunt Barbara said disapprovingly. She turned to Evan. "It is a respectable assembly room where girls of good birth go to meet eligible men."

"I see," Evan said. I could see him trying not to smile.

"Only the very best of the *ton* are admitted," Aunt Barbara went on. "One must have a voucher from one of the patronesses. Fortunately I number Lady Sefton among my acquaintances. She will give me vouchers for Lizzie and Julia."

I said in my haughtiest voice, "My mother was a patroness. Of course we will get vouchers."

Aunt Barbara turned a gimlet gaze on me. "Just make certain you don't do anything that might cast a stain upon the family name, Julia."

I narrowed my eyes but before I could reply Evan said, "If my uncle's behavior couldn't stain the holy name of Marshall, then I hardly think anything Julia might do could place it in jeopardy, Aunt."

That wasn't what I was going to say, but it was satisfactory, and I gave him an approving nod.

*

The next day Aunt Barbara informed us that she had hired a dancing master to teach Lizzie, Evan and me the quadrille and the waltz. Evan tried to get out of it by declaring he had no intention of dancing at any of the affairs he was being dragged to. He would watch, he said.

I thought this was distinctly unfair and told him that it would look ridiculous if he accompanied us to dances and didn't dance himself. "You don't want people thinking Americans are so barbarian that they don't even know how to dance, do you?"

My arrow hit home and he reluctantly agreed to submit to the instruction of Mr. Martelli along with Lizzie and me.

Two days later the dancing master arrived. Grantly escorted him to the ballroom, with its wide expanse of empty bare wooden floor, where we waited with Aunt Barbara. There was a piano in one corner of the ballroom, and she took a seat, indicating she was ready to play. Maria sat on a chair in the corner, prepared to be entertained.

Mr. Martelli was a slender man, with very black hair and very white teeth. He flashed the teeth at us in a smile and said, with a distinct foreign accent, "I am so happy to make your acquaintance. It is an honor for me to be the instructor of such noble and lovely people."

Evan and I looked at each other.

Mr. Martelli fixed his slightly protruding dark eyes upon Evan. "My lord, since you are new to England I suggest we begin with the approach of the gentleman to the lady, and his address to her. The address is like the dance itself – it must be done with grace and élan. You understand?"

"I'm not sure," Evan said cautiously.

"You watch me," Mr. Martelli said to Evan. "I show how to do." He began to approach Lizzie walking on the balls of his feet, his smile still affixed to his face. He stopped in front of her and said to Evan, "When a gentleman requests of a young lady the favor of dancing with her, he should, at the time of addressing her, make his bow, and also request the approbation of the elderly person who may have the charge of her. The bow, it is so." He pointed to his feet. "Watch. One foot takes the second position, the other the third," he arranged his feet with balletic precision, "then the body gently falls forward, keeping the head in a direct line with the body." Mr. Martelli's body tilted toward Lizzie. "As you see, the bend is made by a motion at the union of the inferior limbs with the body."

Evan's face was perfectly grave as he asked, "The 'inferior limbs?' Do you mean the legs?"

Mr. Martelli straightened up. He gave Evan a puzzled look, then his smile appeared again. "Ah, you jest. Americans like the jest, eh?"

Aunt Barbara called from the piano, "For heaven's sake, Mr. Martelli, let us get to the dancing!"

"Of course, of course," said the ever-amiable dancing master. "We shall begin then, eh? Will all of the noble pupils come out on the floor?"

The lesson in the quadrille proceeded fairly smoothly as all of the noble pupils were well coordinated and had an ear for music. I actually found myself having fun. The quadrille needed four couples to make up a set, and we only had two, but after a half an hour we all felt we could participate in a quadrille without disgracing ourselves.

Next, it was time to learn the waltz. "First," said Mr. Martelli, "I will demonstrate by myself." He nodded to Aunt Barbara at the piano and, as the music swept through the room, the dancing master elevated his arms, as if he was clasping a partner, and began to swoop around the floor. "See," he said, "you must count your steps, turning one half a revolution every three counts." He whirled around and around chanting, "One—two—three; one—two—three."

I wondered how he kept from being dizzy. Finally he stopped. "Now, I try it with one of the young ladies." He looked hopefully at Lizzie.

"I'll go first," she obligingly said.

The two faced each other, hands clasped, Mr. Martelli's other hand on Lizzie's waist, Lizzie's other hand on his shoulder. This certainly was different, I thought. In no other dance did one stand in such close proximity to one's partner.

It didn't take Lizzie long to catch on and she and Mr. Martelli were soon twirling around the room in time to the music. It looked like fun.

"Good going, Lizzie," Evan cheered her from the sidelines. His face, as he watched her, was alight with warmth and amusement. My eyes went back to my dancing cousin. Lizzie was really quite amazingly beautiful, I thought.

Then it was my turn to twirl around with Mr. Martelli. It felt very odd being held so close to a man, and I stepped on his toes once or twice.

He kept on smiling gamely. "Not to worry. Not to worry. It happens all the time when one is starting out."

I finally relaxed and let him lead me and soon we were flying around the ballroom in decent harmony. It really was fun.

Then it was Evan's turn. "Are *we* going to dance together?" he asked Mr. Martelli. His mouth was sober, but his blue eyes gleamed with humor.

"Yes, yes, that is how we will start out. Then you can try it with one of the ladies."

With a straight face Evan clasped Mr. Martelli's hand and put his other hand around the dancing master's slender waist. "So," said Mr. Martelli, "we start."

At the sight of the tall Viking that was Evan spinning around with the slender dancing master, I lost my gravity. I started to laugh and couldn't stop. Lizzie joined in, and Maria starting giggling too.

"How am I doing?" Evan called to us as he swooped around with Mr. Martelli.

"Wonderful," Lizzie called back.

"Woops," said Evan. "Sorry."

He had stepped on Mr. Martelli's toe.

"Not to worry," the dancing master said gamely, trying not to wince.

Aunt Barbara stopped playing and the two men came to a halt. "Now you try with the ladies," Mr. Martelli said.

Evan made a face. "I hope I don't step on their toes."

"I'll chance it," Lizzie said with a smile, stepping forward. Aunt Barbara hit the keys and Evan and Lizzie began to circle around the room in time to the music. They made a stunning couple, I thought, both so tall and blond and beautiful. Mr. Martelli counted out loud for them as they waltzed—"One two three, one two three…"

After they had gone around the room a few times, Aunt Barbara stopped playing. "That was very nice," she said approvingly, looking at her daughter, who danced as if she was floating.

"Much more fun dancing with Lizzie than with Mr. Martelli," Evan said humorously.

Lizzie curtseyed. "Thank you, Cousin."

Aunt Barbara said, "You go next, Julia."

All of my amusement fled and suddenly I was nervous. *This is ridiculous*, I told myself as I moved slowly onto the floor to join Evan. *Nobody cares if you make a mistake. There is absolutely no reason to be nervous.*

I lifted my chin and tried to look confident as I came to a stop in front of Evan. He took my hand into his and then his other hand came to rest intimately on my waist. I reached up high to place my hand on his shoulder. Lizzie's height had suited him better, I thought. I was too short.

The music started and we began to waltz.

We were so close that I could smell his skin and feel the warmth from his body. The closeness of Mr. Martelli had been impersonal. Evan's closeness felt completely different. Truth be told, it was making me feel a little dizzy. Or maybe it was the constant circling.

His hand was so big that it encircled almost half my waist.

We were mismatched in height, but still we were somehow managing to move together as if we were one person, not two. It was so easy to go with him. It was as if I felt him in every fiber of my being.

The music stopped. We stood still for a moment, still in the embrace called for by the dance. I glanced up quickly at his face. He was looking down at me and his face was oddly grave.

"Very nice," Aunt Barbara said.

We dropped our hands and stepped away from each other as if she had reprimanded us.

Evan said, in a hearty voice that sounded a little forced, "Would you like to try it Maria? Do you dare to trust your toes to my ineptitude?"

Maria came toward us, her face bright. "I think you're a wonderful dancer, Evan. You and Julia looked as if you had been dancing together forever."

"Beginner's luck," I said. My voice sounded a little huskier than usual and I cleared my throat.

"Splendid, splendid, splendid," said Mr. Martelli as Evan and Maria sailed around the floor. "Never have I had such excellent pupils."

"We have done very well," Lizzie said with satisfaction. "I don't think that any of us will disgrace ourselves if we attempt the waltz in public."

Aunt Barbara rose from the piano and came to join us. Evan had said something to Maria as they came off the floor and she was laughing up at him.

Aunt Barbara bestowed an approving smile on her daughter, her nieces and her nephew. "A successful morning," she pronounced. "Thank you, Mr. Martelli."

"Yes, thank you very much," Lizzie seconded. "It was great fun."

Evan and I were silent.

Aunt Barbara rang the bell. "I will have Grantly see you out," she said to the dancing master.

After the door had closed behind them, Aunt Barbara said, "Now we must call upon Lady Sefton, and procure vouchers for Almack's. That is where you should make your first appearance. We will have to wait until Julia's clothing is delivered, however. She cannot go anywhere with her present wardrobe."

I brought up the subject that I considered the most important part of my London visit. "The first thing we have to do is buy a horse." I forced myself to look at Evan. "You did say you would."

"I did," he returned equably.

"I want to help pick it out," I said.

"Impossible," said Aunt Barbara. "I have already told you, Julia, that ladies cannot go to Tattersall's. You will just have to tell Evan what you want and let him buy something for you."

"I have picked out all my own horses since I outgrew my first pony," I said fiercely. "And Evan knows about boats, not horses."

Aunt Barbara said in measured tones, "You Cannot Go To Tattersall's." She looked at Evan. "I hope you understand that, Nephew, even if Julia does not."

"I understand, Aunt," Evan said.

I started to reply but, infinitesimally, he shook his head. I stopped.

Lizzie said, "It's a nice day, Julia. Do you and Maria want to go for a walk in the park?"

Maria responded eagerly and after a moment I agreed. I desperately needed some fresh air. And I had to figure out a way to make Evan take me to Tattersalls. Perhaps Maria and Lizzie would have some ideas.

Chapter Fifteen

It was a beautiful early spring day and I was delighted to be getting out of the house. I had hoped Evan would accompany us, but he had an appointment in the city. So it was just Lizzie, Maria and me strolling along the walking paths and admiring the burgeoning green of trees and grass.

"I miss having a dog," I said.

What I really meant was that I missed the country. Spring was so beautiful at Stoverton, with its rich green carpets of grass, its explosion of brilliant flowers, its clouds of exuberant birds. I wouldn't dream of subjecting a dog to life in the city; it would be like a prison for him.

I walked along the path with my sister and my cousin, admiring a bright display of daffodils and inhaling the smell of grass and dirt. The path ran along Rotten Row for a mile or so, and I watched the horses trotting up and down. None of the *ton* were out at this hour, it was all middle class cits, dressed in proper riding clothes but with truly terrible seats. It was obvious that none of them had grown up with horses.

Lizzie and Maria had been chatting and when a brief silence fell between them I said, "I should have brought Isabella to London. I miss riding terribly and God knows what kind of nag Evan will pick out." The injustice of it all burned in my chest. "I can't see why I'm not allowed to choose my own horse. It's just stupid that girls can't go to Tattersall's."

Maria said, "You could always send for Isabella, Julia. I'm sure Evan wouldn't mind. It would save him money, after all."

This was true. And I loved Isabella. But I had to admit that I had been looking forward to the challenge of a new horse—a horse that *I* picked out.

"I suppose I could do that," I muttered in response to Maria's suggestion.

"Could you buy a horse someplace other than Tattersall's?" Lizzie inquired. "Perhaps from a private seller?"

"I don't know any private sellers in London," I returned gloomily. "And I need a horse right now. I can't wait for months, looking around here and there. Besides, I *want* to see Tattersall's. It is *the* place to go to buy any kind of horse. They auction off carriage horses, hacks and hunters as well as racehorses... Sir John told me all about it. It's where he purchased Roderick, his best hunter. I want to go."

Maria and Lizzie exchanged glances.

Lizzie said, "If you go to Tattersall's, Julia, my mother will have a seizure. It really is one of those rigid rules that a girl disregards at her peril. And your behavior reflects on my mother, too, don't forget."

What Lizzie didn't say was that it would reflect upon her as well. If I went to Tattersall's with Evan, I would dish her season as well as mine.

It's so stupid, I thought in frustration.

We walked in silence for a while and I tried to get back into the mood of enjoying the spring. I wasn't having much success, though, when I heard Lizzie say, "If you were a boy, you could go."

I stopped, turned, and stared at my cousin. She stopped as well and looked back at me. "Lizzie," I breathed reverently, "you are a genius."

We were staring at each other in mutual satisfaction when Maria asked, "Why is Lizzie a genius? We all know that you could go to Tattersall's if you were a boy."

"To go to Tattersall's all I have to do is *dress* as a boy," I said with a triumphant smile.

"You wouldn't!" Maria cried.

"Why not?"

"Evan will never take you!"

"There is that," Lizzie said. "If you want to pick out your own horse, you have to go with Evan. He's the one who has to pay. And he has to do the talking too. If you open your mouth everyone will know you're a girl."

Maria said indignantly, "Lizzie, you're as bad as Julia."

"Not quite as bad," Lizzie returned. "I wouldn't do it myself. Well, I don't want to go to Tattersall's. But it's the only way Julia is going to get there."

"You're right," I said.

"My father and brothers would never allow you to do such a thing," Lizzie said, "but Evan is an American. Perhaps he won't realize quite what an...outrageous...thing the *ton* would consider such a masquerade."

My brain was teeming with ideas. "I could disguise myself as a groom, one of those little ones who ride behind their masters in sporting vehicles. No one would think it odd for me to accompany Evan if I was dressed like that."

"Yes, but people would think it odd that you weren't holding his horses," Lizzie pointed out.

I scowled and kicked a small rock on the path in front of me. This had to work. It was such a brilliant idea. I kicked another rock and an idea dawned. "He would need a groom to hold the horse he *buys*, wouldn't he?"

Lizzie frowned thoughtfully. "Yes, I suppose he would."

"Won't there be grooms working for Tattersall's who do that?" Maria asked.

"Evan won't know that," I said. I almost clapped my hands with glee. "He doesn't know a thing about Tattersall's. I'll tell him that he'll be expected to come accompanied by a groom, and that the groom will be me. He'll think it's all very natural."

Maria objected. "I don't think you're being fair to Evan. He's been so nice to us, Julia. Suppose you get found out and he gets blamed? That would be a rotten way to repay him for all he's doing for us."

"But don't you see? That's what's so perfect about this," I said. "Evan doesn't give the snap of his fingers for the opinion of the English *ton.* All he wants to do is negotiate a mortgage on Stoverton, pay off our father's debts, and sail home to America. No one in America will know what he's done. Nor will anyone care!"

"I don't know," Maria said unhappily. "You always make the most outrageous things you do sound reasonable. But this isn't reasonable, Julia. It's…oh, I don't know what to call it."

"It's a masquerade," Lizzie said. "The *ton* holds masquerades all the time. This one is just a little more adventurous, that's all."

I grinned. "You *are* as bad as I am, Lizzie."

Lizzie's light blue eyes glimmered. "You're so much fun, Julia. I'm glad we're having this season together."

"You're fun too," I returned. And I meant it. I had always thought that Lizzie would be just like her mother. I pictured Aunt Barbara's face if she knew what Lizzie was recommending and grinned.

"Where will you get the clothes?" she asked practically.

This was a good question. The stables at Althorpe house held Aunt Barbara's four carriage horses, my father's four, and Baron. Aunt Barbara had a groom to look after hers and I had Toby's nephew Sammy looking after mine. Sammy was small. Like me.

"Do you have any money?" I asked Lizzie.

"I still have some of my pin money left."

"If you let me have it, I'll give it to Sammy if he lends me his extra set of clothes for the day. He'll do it. He's Toby's nephew, after all."

"You have to look the part," Lizzie warned. "You can't get caught, Julia. That would be disastrous."

"I won't get caught," I said. "I promise."

"What if Evan doesn't agree?" Maria asked.

"I'll make him agree."

Maria rolled her eyes but didn't answer. She knew it was futile to try to change my mind.

*

The first thing I did when we got home was pay a visit to the stable and have a chat with Sammy, who was happy to loan me his extra clothes in exchange for the remains of Lizzie's pin money. Within a short time I was possessed of a package containing a shirt, breeches, boots, jacket and hat. I raced back to my room to try them on.

The clothes were new, having been bought when Sammy was hired to come with us to London, so I didn't have any unpleasant dirt or smell to deal with. I put the tan breeches on first and they fit fairly well. My legs are longer than you would think in relation to my height. The jacket sleeves were too long, but I tucked them under. The hat had a peak, which was good because I could pull it low to hide my face. It was also full enough to allow me to stuff my hair under it. The boots, however, were too big.

How could someone as small as Sammy have such big feet? I grumbled as I tried to walk around the room in the cumbersome footwear. Perhaps if I stuff some paper into the toes it will stabilize them.

I tried this idea and, while far from perfect, I decided it would have to do. My own boots would look too small for a boy.

I was still in my costume when I heard a knock on my door. "Who is it?" I called cautiously.

"It's us, Lizzie and Maria," Lizzie called back. "We're alone."

"Come in," I said. "Quickly."

The girls scuttled into the room, shutting the door behind them. The two of them stopped dead and stared at me as I posed in front of the fireplace.

Lizzie began to laugh. "You look perfect," she said.

"Thank you," I replied modestly.

Maria almost wailed, "I wish you wouldn't do this, Julia."

I went to her and put an arm around her. "Maria, darling, nothing bad is going to happen. You shouldn't be so afraid all the time. Sometimes you have to take chances if you want to be happy."

"If you want to have your own way, you mean," Maria retorted.

I grinned and began to walk around the room. "These breeches are wonderful. One feels so free, so unfettered." I strode back and forth across the floor a few times, trying to get the knack of walking in the big boots. "It's so unfair that girls have to wear dresses."

"I like my dresses," Lizzie said. "They're much looser and more comfortable than those horrible high neck cloths that men have to wear. I hate the feeling of something close around my neck. I always feel as if it's choking me."

"I suppose that's true," I replied as I continued to pace the floor.

Maria said, "When are you going to ask Evan? If he doesn't agree, you're dished, Julia."

"I'll ask him as soon as he gets home. Grantly said he was going into the city to meet with some solicitor."

"We should go downstairs to wait for him," Lizzie advised.

"All right," I returned. "Go ahead and I'll meet you in the drawing room after I've changed."

Chapter Sixteen

Evan's appointment in the city was with Mr. Rothschild, the solicitor Roger Spenser had recommended. They had a long and fruitful discussion, and, when Evan left Simon Rothschild's office, he felt there was a real chance he would be able to sell the art in the London house. If he could sell those valuable paintings, he'd realize enough money to considerably lower the debts his uncle had left.

If he got Julia settled, he could be on a ship for America by June.

He had written a long letter to his sister Frances explaining his dilemma and apologizing for his delay in returning home. Not that she needed him to run the business; she and John had been doing that well enough for years. Evan had done his part by investing a great deal of his own money in the company, but he felt guilty about his protracted absence.

He was thinking nostalgically about how delightfully simple life was in America when he walked into his palatial London establishment. A footman was there to take his hat. The fellow probably did nothing more all day than stand in the hall waiting to take people's hats. What kind of useless job was that for a man? People could perfectly well place their own hats on the table.

It's ridiculous, he thought grumpily as he started toward the library.

Suddenly Lizzie appeared at the door of the main drawing room. "Evan, might I see you for a moment please?" she said. As he started toward her she disappeared back inside. When he reached the door he almost bumped into Lizzie and Maria, who were on their way out. Lizzie favored him with a bright smile while Maria gave him a strange, anxious look, muttered a greeting, and whisked past him.

He looked toward the fireplace and saw Julia standing there. He frowned. "Is something wrong?"

111

"Not at all," she replied. She gestured to one of the elegant gilt chairs that lined the wall. "Sit down. I have something to ask you."

His grumpiness was displaced by curiosity. He took the seat she had designated and waited to be told.

She came to sit on the chair next to him, turning so she faced him. She was wearing one of her old dresses as the new ones had not yet been delivered, and her hands were tightly clasped in her faded muslin lap. For the first time since he had known her, she looked uncertain.

He said encouragingly, "Yes?"

She lifted her chin and her expression became resolute. "You know how much I want to go to Tattersall's with you to pick out my horse."

He sighed. "Yes, Julia, I know. But I think we have to respect the superior knowledge of Aunt Barbara in this matter. It would cause a scandal if you went to Tattersall's." He added, speaking slowly and clearly, "I do not wish to cause a scandal and wreck Lizzie's season."

She leaned a little toward him, her gray eyes fixed on his face. "It would cause a scandal if I went to Tattersall's dressed as a girl. But what if everyone thought I was a boy?"

It took him a moment to digest what she had just said. She kept gazing at him, steely determination in her extraordinary eyes.

"Are you proposing to dress up as a boy?" he asked cautiously.

"Yes. I borrowed some clothes from Sammy, and they fit perfectly. No one need ever know who I am."

Evan felt an almost irresistible desire to laugh. But she was too serious, too determined, for him to do that to her. So he schooled his face to gravity and said, "I see."

"I'll stand right next to you the whole time," she said. "It's an auction and if I see a horse I want you to bid on, I'll just touch your coat. No one will know that you're taking instructions from me. I won't talk at all."

He regarded her skeptically. How could anyone look at that face and think she was a boy?

He said, "Your eyes are a very unusual color, Julia. Suppose someone who sees you with me at the auction meets you again in a ballroom? Won't he suspect?"

"I have a hat with a peak and I can pull it down low over my forehead. And I won't look at anyone, Evan! I promise. The costume is perfect. No one will know."

He was silent.

She drew a deep, resolute breath and said bravely, "Please?"

Why shouldn't she pick out her own horse? he thought. She knows a hell of a lot more about horses than I do. She hated coming to London. At least she should have a horse to ride.

"I'd like to see you in this outfit before I make up my mind," he said.

Her face lit with joy and he blinked. Julia happy was a beautiful sight. He would like to see her look like that more frequently.

"I'll try it on for you," she said. "Where can we go?"

"My bedroom has a dressing room attached," he said. "You can use that."

"I'll go upstairs and get the clothes," she said. "Wait here." She almost ran out the door.

He got up from the sofa and walked over to one of the windows, which looked out on a line of Greek-style columns. He scarcely saw the elegant columns, however. In his mind's eye he was seeing Julia's face.

He had never met a girl who was as unaware of her looks as Julia. She seemed to have no idea of how beautiful she was. Once she was cleaned up and dressed properly, he had no doubt she would have plenty of men interested in marrying her—especially with the handsome dowry he planned to offer.

He frowned. He would have to make certain that the dowry was tied up in a way that couldn't be abused by her husband. He made a mental note to consult with Mr. Rothschild about that.

The door opened and Julia was there, a bundle of clothes clutched to her chest. He got up and said, "Come along and we'll see what you look like."

They went down the hall to the earl's apartment, which was enormous. Evan had been shocked to see that it had two bedrooms, each with an attached dressing room. At home married couples slept in the same room. In the same bed. Then he had thought, *Of course, if you married for money or social status, and not for love, you might want to have your own space.*

He thought a marriage like that would be nothing but a misery.

As they reached his door, it occurred to him that bringing Julia into his bedroom would be considered very improper, even in America. He said, "Perhaps we should go into the Countess' bedroom instead. There is a dressing room there as well."

"Don't be silly," she said impatiently. "No one is going to know."

"All right." He opened his bedroom door and stood aside to let her enter.

It was a more opulent room than his bedchamber at Stoverton had been, with tapestry bed hangings and silk-covered walls. At least there was a seascape he quite liked hanging over the mantelpiece.

Julia immediately headed for the dressing room. Evan sat in one of the chairs in front of the marble fireplace and waited. She didn't take long.

"Well," she said, standing before him and regarding him a little anxiously. "What do you think? Isn't it a good disguise?"

He tried very hard to regard her as a boy. He tried not to look at her surprisingly long elegant legs, which didn't look remotely masculine. He forced his eyes to move downward. "Your feet have grown, I see," he managed to get out.

"I know. I had to stuff paper in the toes. But I can manage. Just watch." She paraded back and forth in front of him, frowning a little in concentration. "See."

She would never look like a boy to him. But she wanted this so much. If they got found out, well, they would deal with the consequences. He just didn't have it in him to deny her.

"You look fine," he said. "Just make sure that no one gets a look at your eyes."

She nodded eagerly. "I will be very careful, Evan. Then you'll do it?"

He sighed. "Yes."

She actually jumped up and down in her excitement. It was a nice feeling, making Julia happy.

"Sale days at Tattersall's are Monday and Thursday," she said. "Today is Wednesday. Do you think we could go tomorrow?"

"No point in waiting," he said resignedly.

"Do you know what, Evan?" she said with a burst of feeling. "I'm *glad* you're an American! No Englishman would have the nerve to do this."

"Well," he said with a crooked smile, "I do think you should be allowed to pick out your own horse."

Chapter Seventeen

Evan left it to Julia to get away from their aunt; he had no doubt that her fertile imagination would come up with something.

Sure enough, at breakfast, when Lady Barbara announced her intention of taking the girls shopping for gloves and hair ribbons, Julia announced that she was not feeling well and thought she should spend the day in bed.

Evan saw the look that passed between Lizzie and Maria. *They know,* he thought with amusement as the two girls turned solemn faces to Lady Barbara. Lizzie said, "Yes, you mentioned last night that you weren't feeling well. The feeling hasn't passed?"

"No," Julia said regretfully.

Evan thought that for a sick person she had certainly eaten an inordinate amount of breakfast, but forbore to voice this observation to his aunt.

Lady Barbara frowned at Julia. "What is wrong?"

"My stomach is upset."

Lady Barbara's frown deepened. "Then you should not have eaten so much breakfast."

"I know," Julia said mournfully. She put her hand to her mouth, rolled her eyes, muttered, "Excuse me," and ran from the table.

"I'll go with her," Lizzie said, jumping to her feet.

There was a tight line around Lady Barbara's mouth. "The new clothes are to be delivered this afternoon and I have made an appointment to visit Lady Sefton tomorrow. It is imperative that Julia come with us. Lady Sefton is one of the patronesses of Almack's and Julia must be presented to her." She stared across the table at Evan, her blue eyes imperative. "You are to come as well, Evan. It is essential that you make your bow to one of society's most important hostesses."

Evan looked thoughtful. "Now, how did Mr. Martelli show me that bow?"

Maria giggled.

Lady Barbara was not amused. "If your new clothes are not ready, then you will have to come in your old ones. But I will be taking the girls to Almack's next week and I require you to accompany us. You absolutely must have your evening dress by then."

"Yes, ma'am," Evan said. He glanced at Maria, who was drinking her tea. "Have you found someone to look after Maria, Aunt? I don't want her left alone with the servants while the rest of us go out to parties."

"I know. I know. I have not forgotten; I have just been very busy. I will have one of the agencies in town send over a few people for me to interview."

He gave her a steady look. "I want Maria to meet this governess before you hire her. I don't want her saddled with someone she doesn't like."

Lady Barbara bristled. "A young girl is hardly the best judge of a governess's qualifications, Evan. I believe that you may safely leave that up to me."

Evan said imperturbably, "You can judge the qualifications, but Maria must judge the personality. It has to be someone she likes."

Lady Barbara glared down at the piece of toast on her plate. *How did such an ill-tempered woman produce a sweet-natured girl like Lizzie?* Evan thought in wonder.

He glanced at Maria and she mouthed the words, *Thank you* to him.

You're welcome, he mouthed back.

*

After the shopping party had left, Julia made an appearance in the library, where Evan was frowning at the stack of bills that had come in from various clothing shops on Bond Street. He looked up as she came into the room.

"Have you decided how to get away from the house without the servants knowing?" he asked affably.

Of course she had a ready answer. "I have a long pelisse I can wear over Sammy's clothes. I'll carry his hat and boots and change in the carriage on the way to Tattersall's. No one will ever know."

No one will ever know. Julia seemed to be saying that quite frequently these days. He devoutly hoped she was right. If she ruined all her chances of having a season by this adventure, he didn't know what he was going to do with her.

I suppose I could marry her myself.

Without warning the shocking words popped into his head. Good God, he thought in horror. What am I thinking? Julia and me? It's impossible. We're first cousins!

"Evan?" she was saying. "What do you think of my plan?"

He pulled his attention back to her inquiring face. "It's as good as any, I suppose. Does this mean we have to take the carriage and not the curricle?"

"Yes. I don't want to chance anyone seeing me changing my shoes and my hat."

"Have you come up with an idea about how to square the coachman?"

"We have to take Papa's carriage anyway, because Aunt Barbara took hers. Sammy will drive—he won't give me away."

He sighed. "All right. I'll order the carriage for a half an hour from now. Can you be ready by then?"

She gave him a brilliant smile. "Of course. I'll meet you in the front hall in half an hour's time."

He nodded and looked back at the bills on his desk.

After she had gone, he sat thinking for a moment of that treacherous notion that had flashed so unexpectedly into his mind. I feel sorry for her, he reasoned. She's so gallant and she's so alone. I hope we can find her a good husband.

He resolutely squashed the feeling of dismay that came over him at the thought of Julia's marrying someone else.

A footman came in the door and announced that a representative from Barings Bank was there to see him.

"Show the gentleman in," Evan said.

*

Evan spent more time with the gentleman from Barings than he had anticipated and was late meeting Julia in the front hall. She scowled at him as he made his appearance.

"The carriage has been waiting for fifteen minutes!"

"I'm sorry. I was speaking to someone from the bank. They're prepared to take back a mortgage on Stoverton."

"Oh."

"It has to be done, Julia." He didn't say anything to her about his meeting with Simon Rothschild. He wanted to make sure the entail could be broken before he broached that subject.

"Yes. I know." Her voice was so low that he had to strain to hear it.

"You look perfectly normal," he said approvingly, regarding her long coat and velvet bonnet. "You're dressed a little warmly for such a day, perhaps, but, seeing you, no one would suspect a thing."

The sadness left her face and she grinned at him. "Are you ready? I can hardly wait."

"Let's go, then," he said.

The ubiquitous footman moved forward to open the door and they went out into the April sunshine.

Chapter Eighteen

Tattersall's was another shock to Evan. He had expected a larger version of the horse fair in Boston, but this huge, elegant building, with its Greek-temple style colonnades, its accommodation for a hundred and twenty horses, not to mention the commodious kennel for hounds, looked more like a palace to him than a horse auction house.

A large gathering of men were present, most of them well dressed and prosperous looking. He didn't see anyone else accompanied by a groom. Julia had assured him that everyone would have a groom. He set his teeth and prepared to get through what he suspected would be an excruciating afternoon.

Julia, with her hat pulled well down over her face, was looking around with eager interest. "Let's go see the horses," she whispered to him, tilting her head toward the stables that were placed along one side of the yard.

He nodded and moved in the direction she had indicated. She followed close behind.

For the next hour Evan watched Julia with warm amusement. She was in heaven. She insisted on looking at every horse, the racehorses and the carriage horses as well as the riding horses. The one she fell in love with was a polished chestnut gelding, a thoroughbred with an intelligent face and beautifully arched neck.

Even Evan, admittedly not a horse person, could see the animal's quality. His legs looked straight and sound, his chest was square, and his shoulders sloped at a perfect angle. He was smaller than the other horses that were being shown, but Evan thought a smaller horse would suit Julia.

"This one," she murmured to him when they came back to look at the horse for the second time. The gelding was regarding them curiously and she reached out to pat his neck. He seemed calm and friendly and, as Evan watched, she dexterously opened his mouth to take a quick look at his teeth.

The man looking at the horse next to them gave her a curious glance as she stepped back from the chestnut gelding and Evan said quickly, "Thank you for checking his teeth, Sammy. I don't wish to soil my gloves."

Julia looked guilty and ducked her head respectfully at Evan. Then she slipped around to his other side, using his big body to shield her from the view of the too-curious fellow in front of the other stall.

The gelding was brought to the auction block about halfway through the program. He did move beautifully, Evan thought, as he was trotted around the yard. Julia evidently felt the same because she looked up at Evan, her heart in her eyes, and breathed softly, "He's perfect."

He didn't reply, just kept looking attentively at the horse.

The bidding began and Evan was pleased it wasn't as high as most of the other horses had fetched. He thought perhaps the size of the horse was a factor. He was too small for most men and too much horse for most women.

Evan upped the previous offer to ninety pounds and for a moment there was silence in the yard. The auctioneer said, "Come now, this is a beautiful horse with excellent breeding, warranted sound, without fault or blemish. Do I hear another bid?"

From the other side of the ring a new voice called out. "One hundred pounds."

"One hundred and ten," Evan said.

"One twenty," came the other voice.

Evan felt Julia stiffen beside him. He glanced at her agonized face and determined he would buy this damn horse no matter how much he had to spend.

"One thirty," said Evan.

"One thirty-five," the other bidder called. His voice sounded determined.

The bidding continued to rise. The rest of the men at the auction were looking with open curiosity at the two men as the bidding went ever higher.

"It's a nice little horse," the man next to Evan growled to his companion. "But surely it's not worth this kind of price?"

"One hundred and ninety pounds," the opposing bidder said.

The auctioneer didn't have time to ask for another offer before Evan said firmly, "Two hundred pounds."

There was silence on the other side of the ring.

Next to him Julia gave a little jump of excitement.

"Do I hear another bid?" the auctioneer said.

"No," the opposing bidder replied. "I'm done."

"Then sold to the gentleman for two hundred pounds," the auctioneer said and banged his gavel.

Julia looked radiant. Evan bent and murmured, "Pull that hat further over your face and keep your eyes down!"

She obeyed hastily.

He made the arrangements for payment and delivery. They were walking toward their carriage when a slender, elegant looking gentleman in well-cut riding clothes stopped Evan. "You were determined to buy that horse," the man said pleasantly. Evan recognized the voice of the man who had bid against him.

"Yes," Evan replied with equal pleasantness. "I liked him."

"I believe you are the new Earl of Althorpe," the man said. "I have seen you before. I am Ormesby. No doubt we shall be meeting again at some affair or other."

"How do you do," Evan said, holding out his hand. "Sorry I took your horse, but I want him for my cousin. She needs a horse to ride while she's in London."

"Well, if he doesn't suit and you want to resell him, let me know."

"I will," Evan responded.

Ormesby gave Julia a curious glance. "I see you brought your groom with you."

"Yes," Evan replied easily. "I thought that perhaps I would have to bring the horse home with me, but it seems they will deliver."

The man nodded. "Well, good day. Good luck with the horse."

"Thank you," Evan replied.

The two men parted and Julia followed Evan back to the carriage. Neither of them spoke until the horses were in motion. Then Evan said grimly, "I hope no one was watching us depart. They will think it very odd that my groom rides inside the carriage with me."

Julia turned to him. "Oh, Evan! *Thank you!* I can't believe you paid all that money for him! But he's worth it. He's a beautiful, beautiful horse. I already love him."

He looked down at her as she sat beside him and she gave him a brilliant smile. "I never thought you would go so high. You shouldn't have gone so high. But I'm glad you did!"

He said gently, "I can't give you back what your father took from you, but at least I can give you a horse."

They looked at each other for a long moment and Evan felt something leap between them. Then Julia flushed and moved a little away from him. She said in a small, formal voice, "It is very kind of you and I deeply appreciate it."

He looked at her boots. "You had better change back into your own gear."

"Yes."

She bent over to unlace Sammy's boots and replace them with her own. When she sat back up again and was tying the bow of her bonnet, he said cheerfully, "Have you thought of a name?"

"No." She finished tying her bow and turned to him. "He's such a beautiful color."

"He is. Would you say he's red?"

"More like a red-gold."

"Mmm," he nodded agreement. "It's the same color as the woman's hair in the picture you have by that fellow Titian."

"That's perfect," Julia said with delight. "I'll call him Titian. Ty for short."

He looked pleased. "I like that."

She nodded firmly. "I like it too. She spent the rest of the trip home extolling the perfections of her new horse.

Chapter Nineteen

I made it safely upstairs in my bonnet and pelisse and was just opening the door to my room when Aunt Barbara emerged from Lizzie's room and saw me.

"Where have you been, Julia?" she demanded. "Grantly told me you and Evan had gone out in that dilapidated old carriage. I thought you were feeling ill."

Damn, I thought.

Lizzie came into the hallway as well.

I pulled my pelisse around me tightly and said, "I felt that some air would do me good, so Evan was kind enough to take me out. We used the carriage and opened the window and it made me feel much better."

Lady Barbara looked skeptical. "A carriage ride is an unusual cure for an upset stomach."

"It might be unusual, but it worked," I replied.

Aunt Barbara eyed me suspiciously.

Lizzie said hurriedly, "Our new clothes have arrived, Julia! Nancy has hung yours in your wardrobe. Don't you want to see? I'll come in with you."

A footman appeared in the hallway. "My lady, a Miss Hood is here to see you. About the governess position, I believe."

"Very good, Sidney," Lady Barbara returned. "Put her in the Blue Salon and I will be there shortly."

"Yes, my lady."

"You're interviewing governesses for Maria?" I asked.

"Yes."

"I hope you'll give Maria a chance to meet whomever you select before you hire her. Maria isn't difficult to please, but her wishes should be consulted. She's not a little girl, after all."

"Your cousin has made that abundantly clear to me," Lady Barbara said acidly. "Maria will be consulted."

Lizzie and I watched as Lady Barbara moved down the passageway. When she had disappeared from sight we went into my room.

"Well," Lizzie said as soon as the door had closed. "Did you do it? Did you buy a horse?"

I put my package containing Sammy's boots and hat down on the bed. "We did. He's so beautiful, Lizzie! I can't wait to ride him!"

Lizzie sat down on the bed next to the package. "Tell me all," she demanded.

I sat down next to her and enthusiastically complied.

*

At dinner that evening, Evan told Aunt Barbara that he had purchased a horse for me. "It's being delivered tomorrow morning," he said. "I hope Julia will be pleased."

Aunt Barbara's eyes narrowed. "How did you go to Tattersall's if you were out in the carriage with Julia all afternoon?"

I searched frantically for an answer to this very cogent question but before I could come up with anything Evan came to the rescue. "I went earlier in the day to choose the horse and a friend was kind enough to stay and do the bidding for me."

"Tattersall's can be very expensive," Aunt Barbara commented.

"Indeed," Evan returned enigmatically.

"What friend did you ask to bid for you?"

Evan lifted his eyebrows. "I doubt you would know him, Aunt."

Aunt Barbara looked unsatisfied, but she couldn't pursue the question any longer without appearing rude.

"I did make one new acquaintance while I was there," Evan said. "A Mr. Ormesby. Do you know him, Aunt?"

"*Mr.* Ormesby?"

"Well, he introduced himself as 'Ormesby'."

"Good heavens. You must mean the *Marquis* of Ormesby. A young man, slim with black hair?"

"That was he," Evan agreed.

"Good heavens." Aunt Barbara's eyes shone. "Ormesby is one of the biggest catches on the marriage mart, girls. Large estates, plenty of money. He has made a name for himself in the government—I believe he is considered one of Lord Castlereagh's most trusted lieutenants. Altogether a most suitable young man for you to know."

"How young is he?" I inquired curiously. The marquis had not looked that young to me.

"He must be in his early thirties," Aunt Barbara answered.

Lizzie said, "I wonder he isn't married by now."

I found this remark puzzling and said so.

"A marquis' first duty is to provide an heir to his name and property." Lizzie smiled at me. "For such a duty to be accomplished, he needs a wife. Most men in his position are married in their twenties."

Aunt Barbara provided us with the answer to Lizzie's question. "The present marquis is a younger brother who inherited the title quite recently. The elder brother unfortunately perished of a putrid infection of the lungs, leaving only daughters. That is why the present marquis is still unwed." She gave her daughter a teasing smile. "Perhaps that will be to your benefit, Lizzie."

Lizzie smiled demurely.

"I think it's so unfair that girls cannot inherit from their fathers," I said.

"I agree with you," Evan returned wholeheartedly. "I would much rather you owned Stoverton than I, Julia." He lifted his eyebrows in a gesture I was coming to recognize. "If this was America, I might add, you would have inherited."

"If your sister Frances had been an only child, would your father have left her the entire shipping company?"

"Of course he would have. Frances is the eldest and she's extremely competent."

"Well, that's one good thing about America, I must admit," I said.

He grinned at me across the table and I felt that smile all the way down to my stomach. Hastily I turned to my aunt, who was saying, "I will invite the marquis to our ball. He is definitely a *parti* you girls should meet."

I did my best to smile demurely like Lizzie.

Chapter Twenty

The following day I wanted to wait at home for Ty to be delivered, but Aunt Barbara insisted that we pay a visit to Lady Sefton. So, reluctantly dressed in my fine new clothes, I got in the carriage with my aunt, Lizzie and Evan to be taken to Grosvenor Square.

Lady Sefton's house fronted directly on the square, with no imposing gates to shield it from the street. One simply got out of one's carriage, walked up the stairs and knocked on the door. Which is what we did.

Lady Sefton's butler ushered us into the drawing room where she awaited us. The first thing I noticed was the painting over the marble fireplace. It was the portrait of a woman with powdered hair, a low-cut blue gown, a fan and a spaniel. Her brown eyes had a knowing look and there was an air of great sophistication about the entire painting. *Sir Joshua Reynolds*, I thought. We had one of his paintings at Stoverton hanging in the long gallery and I recognized the style.

Lady Sefton rose to greet us. She was a sweet-looking woman who bestowed a warm smile upon Aunt Barbara and invited us to be seated.

It was immediately obvious that Lady Sefton was impressed by Evan. As well she should be, I thought with satisfaction. He is the best of the Marshalls. I then had the most disconcerting feeling that in thinking this I was betraying the first earl.

Lady Sefton had finally finished questioning Evan about America and turned her attention to Lizzie and me.

"You girls must be so excited that Lord Byron will be living across the street from you," she said with a sparkle of excitement.

Lizzie's eyes opened wide. "No! Is he really?"

"I have it on the best authority that he has taken Devonshire House for the season. He and his new wife should be in residence any day now, I expect."

"How thrilling," Lizzie said. Her blue eyes were bright. "I have read all his poems."

I said, "I've never heard of him. Who is he?"

The three other women in the room stared at me with open-mouthed incredulity.

"I've never heard of the fellow either," Evan put in, backing me up.

"He's a famous poet," Lizzie finally managed to say.

"He's probably as famous for his bad behavior as he is for his poetry," Aunt Barbara said, looking down her nose. "I am not pleased by the thought of his living across the street from me."

"He's a married man, now," Lady Sefton said. "We must hope his bad behavior is behind him."

Lizzie said, "How is it that you've never heard of him, Julia? You're such a great reader."

I said with dignity, "I haven't had any new books for a while."

Evan said, "We'll stop at a bookshop and buy you a copy of this Byron fellow's poems, Julia. You should probably have a look at them."

"You must read 'The Corsair,' Lady Julia," Lady Sefton urged. "All of the *ton* is mad for it. Just fancy, it sold ten thousand copies on the first day of publication."

"Ten thousand copies!" Evan looked impressed.

"'There was a laughing devil in his sneer,'" Lizzie quoted soulfully.

Evan's impressed look faded. It faded even further as Lizzie continued:

> *That raised emotions both of rage and fear;*
>
> *And where his frown of hatred darkly fell,*
>
> *Hope withering fled—and Mercy sighed farewell!*

"Good God," Evan said. "Is that how he writes?"

Aunt Barbara said, "I believe he is more admired by women than by men."

I suppressed a smile at the expression on Evan's face. He might not know much about art, I thought, but he can certainly recognize bad poetry.

Evan was saying, "My own favorite poet is Shakespeare, and somehow I doubt that this Byron fellow is going to supplant him in my esteem."

I was delighted by this declaration. "I adore Shakespeare," I said enthusiastically. "One can never tire of reading him."

Our eyes met in pleased recognition.

"I always have a copy of his plays on shipboard. He has such amazing insight into the human condition."

I thought this was a very perceptive comment.

Lady Sefton said, "You will enjoy the theatre here in London, then, my lord. Mr. Kean has been delighting us with his performances. I believe he is to perform *The Merchant of Venice* this year at Drury Lane."

"We'll have to go," Evan said.

"What fun," Lizzie said.

When we rose to leave a few minutes later, I tucked Evan's comment about going to the theatre into my memory. That was a promise I would hold him to.

*

Ty was waiting for me when we arrived home. I quickly changed into riding clothes and ran to the stable to meet him.

He was just as beautiful as I remembered. I examined him all over, fed him carrots, stroked his face and talked to him. He listened with ears pricked, as if he understood every word I said. I was dying to ride him and when Evan arrived to see Ty as well, I said, "I want to try him out but I can't go by myself. It's absurd, but according to Aunt Barbara girls can't go anywhere by themselves in London. Will you come with me to Hyde Park?"

Evan frowned. "You haven't even sat on this horse yet, Julia. Are you sure you want to take him through the city streets?"

"I would rather take him through the woods at Stoverton," I said agreeably. "But I don't have that choice, do I?"

"This is the busiest time of day in the streets. Why don't you wait until tomorrow and we can go out early in the morning, before the traffic has time to build up?"

"You bought him for me so I would have a horse to ride in London! Now you're telling me that I can't ride him? That's not fair, Evan!"

He let out a long breath. "Put a saddle on him and ride him around the courtyard first. Let's see how he handles."

It was a matter of minutes before my beautiful Ty was tacked up. I swung up into my comfortable old sidesaddle and picked up my reins.

How are you doing, fellow? I asked him through the reins.

Energy flowed back to me, but he stood quietly. I squeezed him lightly with my calf and he immediately stepped forward into the bit. He had a wonderful walk, very forward and free. His small, elegant ears flicked backwards, listening to me. I asked him to trot.

It was the trot I had seen at Tattersall's, very long, very forward.

I can't believe this horse wasn't being sold as a hunter, I thought. They probably thought he was too small. I wish I could put him over some fences.

I didn't want to stop, but Evan was waiting patiently for me in front of the stable. When I pulled up in front of him, he was smiling. "You look grand together," he said.

"He's wonderful!" I beamed back at him. "How can I ever thank you for buying me this magnificent horse?"

"You can thank me by trying to enjoy your social acquaintances with a little bit of the enthusiasm you show for your horse," he answered dryly.

"I am going to be so good, Evan," I said earnestly. "I will be nice to everyone. I promise." I patted Ty on his neck. "Now, will you come with me to the park?"

He laughed. "I suppose so." He turned to Sammy, who had been watching me as well. "Can you saddle up Baron for me?"

"Good. I'll go get changed."

Chapter Twenty-One

Julia and Evan's ride to the park was a little more exciting than Evan had hoped. The rumble of the traffic and the noise of people hawking their wares spooked Ty. He snorted, rolled his eyes and gave an occasional buck, but Julia managed to keep him going forward. The bridle path was nearly empty this early in the afternoon and a good hard gallop helped Ty to get rid of his excess energy. Evan was relieved to see he behaved better on the way home.

The expression on Julia's face as she rode the beautiful chestnut tugged at Evan's heart. She rode like an angel and he didn't regret for a moment the two hundred pounds he had paid for Ty. She deserved the best.

When they arrived back at their home stable Julia remained to oversee Ty's grooming and Evan returned to the house to change his clothes. He had left his bedroom and was walking down the hall when he saw a strange young lady standing in the vestibule. A worn-looking portmanteau rested at her feet.

"Hello," he said. "I'm..." he hesitated. It always sounded ridiculous to him when he called himself a lord. "I'm Lord Althorpe," he admitted at last.

"How do you do, my lord," the woman replied in a soft, well-bred voice. "I am Emma Dixon, the new governess."

"Ah," Evan said. He regarded the tall, auburn-haired young lady. "I am very pleased to meet you, Miss Dixon. We have been anxious for Maria to continue her education, and to have a comfortable companion as well."

The new governess smiled. She was a very pretty girl, he thought. She had large, gentle-looking brown eyes, rather like a doe's, and soft brown hair worn in a simple bun on her neck. He estimated her to be in her middle twenties.

"I am happy that Maria chose me," she said. "I liked her very much the one time we met."

Lady Barbara came sailing down the stairs, followed by the housekeeper. "Miss Dixon, you have arrived. Splendid. Mrs. Sales, our housekeeper, will show you to your room. I will tell Maria you are here. and she can show you around the schoolroom."

"Thank you, Lady Barbara," Miss Dixon replied.

"Come along with me, Miss," Mrs. Sales said. "Peter here will carry up your bag."

The footman picked up the bag and followed the two women toward the stairs.

Evan said to his aunt, "She seems a very pleasant young woman."

"A little too young, I think," Lady Barbara said. "She was my last choice, but Maria liked her. Evidently Miss Dixon is very musical."

"Then she will be perfect for Maria. By the way, have you engaged a music teacher for her yet?"

"I am pursuing that," Lady Barbara said. "I have not precisely had a great deal of free time."

Evan responded to the rebuke by saying, "Would you like me to do it?"

Lady Barbara smiled. "My dear Evan, you wouldn't have the least notion of how to go about it."

This was indubitably true, but he wanted Maria to have a music teacher right away and his aunt seemed to be dragging her feet. "Are there agencies for music teachers the way there are agencies for governesses?"

"I have heard Maria play. An ordinary music teacher will not do for her. I will find someone, Evan. I have told a number of my friends I am looking. and I am sure something will come up."

"Thank you, ma'am," he replied, a little chastened. She was doing more than he had given her credit for.

She looked him up and down. "You look very well in your new clothes, Evan. A perfect gentleman."

His new clothes were certainly tighter and less comfortable than his old ones, but he was pleased to have his aunt's infrequent approval. After all, he would not have to wear them forever. Once he set sail for America, he could toss the whole extravagant, uncomfortable wardrobe over the side of the ship. In fact, he looked forward to doing so.

"Where are the girls?" he asked.

"In the library. If you are going there, Evan, will you please tell Maria to go upstairs to welcome Miss Dixon?"

"Certainly." When he reached the library, he found Lizzie and Maria comfortably disposed with books in their hands. He gave Maria her message and she jumped up and went out the door just as Julia was coming in.

Julia said as she advanced into the room. "The new governess is here? Just in time. We have to go to Almack's tomorrow night. Now Maria will have someone to keep her company."

"She seemed like a very nice young woman," Evan said as he looked at Lizzie's book. "What are you reading, Lizzie?"

"Lord Byron's new poem."

Julia groaned. "Again? I read that awful thing last night, Lizzie. How can you bear to waste your time on such nonsense?"

Lizzie said, "Julia, stop complaining about Lord Byron! *Everyone* loves him. Perhaps he does…exaggerate…a little, but that's part of the fun."

Julia plucked the book from her hand and closed it firmly. "It isn't fun. It's terrible poetry. One or two of his lyrics are all right, I suppose, but this *Corsair* thing is dreadful."

Lizzie snatched her book back. "You had better go and change your clothes. Mama doesn't approve of riding clothes in the house."

"I just wanted to get some paper so I can write Sir John a letter about my new horse," Julia said with dignity.

Lizzie warned, "We're going to Almack's tonight, Julia, and I recommend you don't share your opinion of Lord Byron's talent. It won't make you popular."

Julia snorted.

Evan smothered a smile and said, "I confess, I'm not looking forward to Almack's. My aunt has made it sound so...so..."

"Boring," Julia said.

Evan grinned. "Well...yes."

"You are the two most anti-social beings I have ever met," Lizzie said. "What is wrong with going to a dance and meeting new people?"

Evan and Julia looked at each other. Julia was the one to answer first. "I'm going to try, Lizzie, but I really don't know what

I'm supposed to talk about with a bunch of strangers."

"Talk about horses," Evan advised. "You can go on forever with that topic."

"And what are *you* going to talk about?" Julia retorted. "You can't offend everyone by regaling them with your very unflattering opinion of England and the English."

Evan sighed. "I know."

What he didn't say was that the American Minister's secretary, John Wood, had begged him to do his best to charm the English nobles he would be meeting. The Minister himself, John Quincy Adams, though brilliant, had a talent for infuriating people that was unequaled in the diplomatic world. He was rarely invited to social events and Evan could be a useful ambassador for the United States.

Lizzie stood up. "I think we should go and meet Maria's new governess, Julia. It would be polite."

"All right." Julia looked at Evan. "Did you get her name?"

"Emma Dixon."

Lizzie said, "Too bad Maria won't be dining with us anymore. I'll miss her."

Evan frowned. "Why should Maria no longer dine with us?"

"In England schoolroom girls always dine with their governess," Lizzie explained. "Maria has been dining with us because my mother didn't want her to be alone. But that will change now that she has Miss Dixon."

Evan felt Julia look at him. He shot her a quick glance then said to Lizzie, "Maria will continue to dine with her family and Miss Dixon will join us as well. She is an educated young woman and will be an asset to our company."

"Mama won't like it," Lizzie warned.

"I am quite sure she will see my point," Evan replied calmly.

"Of course she will," Julia said. "After all, it *is* Evan's house, Lizzie."

A gleeful light sparkled in Lizzie's celestial blue eyes, but she didn't reply.

Chapter Twenty-Two

The carriage pulled up in front of Almack's and Lizzie and I stared in amazement. The building was positively shabby.

"*This* is Almack's?" Lizzie said to her mother.

"What makes it so exclusive, Elizabeth, is not what is outside, but *who* is inside," Aunt Barbara replied.

One of Aunt Barbara's footmen jumped down from the driver's seat and opened the carriage door for us. Aunt Barbara went first, then Lizzie, then me. Evan came last. He had been sitting next to me in the carriage because, as my aunt said, he was the biggest and I was the smallest.

I had been conscious of him every second of the drive. How big he was. How my shoulder would bump against his arm when the carriage made a turn. Even without looking at him, I could tell when he smiled. I heard it in his voice.

I had a dreadful suspicion I wasn't feeling this way because he reminded me of the first earl.

"Well, *we* certainly look elegant even if our destination does not," Lizzie said, smoothing down her skirt.

This was true. I had been surprised at how different I looked when Lizzie's maid finished with me. My new gown fell gracefully to the top of my soft leather shoes. The scooped neck was a little disconcerting—I had never shown so much flesh in my life—but I thought the long line of the skirt made me look taller. The dress itself had a thin white layer of some gauzy material draped over a pale green underskirt. There was a pale green ribbon tied under my breasts, which were already more noticeable because of the scoop neck. I wore long gloves and a pearl necklace Evan had surprised me with before we left the house.

I looked like a real lady, like a daughter my mother might have been proud of.

Lizzie, of course, looked gorgeous. Her dress was similar to mine only the underskirt was blue, to pick up the blue of her eyes.

She grabbed my hand once, quickly, as we walked toward the door, and I grinned at her.

Evan was wearing the correct evening dress for Almack's, knee breeches and a long black coat with tails, and when he followed us to Almack's front door the street lamp threw its light on his neatly brushed hair, making it look as silvery as the moon itself.

A footman opened the door to this revered temple of matchmaking and we passed into a paneled vestibule, presented our vouchers to Mr. Willis, the host, purchased our tickets, and ascended the stairs to the ballroom.

The dancing had not yet started and as we stood in the door I saw how people turned to look at us. *I am going to hate this*, I thought, but I stuck my chin in the air, took a deep breath and prepared to endure.

Evan bent and said in my ear, "The stable at Stoverton is nicer than this."

I couldn't help it. I laughed. He was right. The empty floor was scuffed and warped looking, in total contrast to all the well-dressed people who stood around it waiting for the music to begin. The walls needed a coat of paint badly.

"Come," Lady Barbara commanded, and we trooped after her to stand before a triumvirate of women, who sat like queens in gilt chairs on the edge of the dance floor. I recognized Lady Sefton, the patroness who had given us our vouchers.

Lady Sefton greeted us with a sweet, friendly smile and introduced Lizzie, Evan and me to the other patronesses enthroned beside her. Lady Jersey gave me a hard stare and said, "So you are Helen Althorpe's daughter. It is nice to meet you, Julia."

I bobbed my head. "Thank you, my lady."

Mrs. Drummond Burrell, looking as if she was smelling something particularly noxious and ignored me, saying to Evan, "One can see right away that you are a Marshall, my lord."

All three ladies had something flattering to say to Aunt Barbara about Lizzie's beauty. One of the things I liked about Lizzie is that she didn't like comments about her looks. Her serene expression never changed as Lady Barbara accepted the compliments.

The orchestra began to tune up, signifying the imminence of the first dance. "We always begin with a minuet," Lady Sefton said, addressing herself to Lizzie and me. "We are permitting the waltz this year, but a young girl must gain our permission before she is allowed to dance it."

These ladies must be desperate for power, I thought. How sad they had to settle for making stupid rules about a dance.

Evan asked politely, "And how does a young girl get your permission to dance the waltz?

The three ladies looked at him with pleasure in their eyes. A quick glance around had told me that he was quite the most splendid looking man in the room.

"Her partner must ask us," Lady Sefton said.

"Every time she wants to waltz?"

Mrs. Drummond Burrell actually smiled at him. "Once she has our permission, she may waltz when she chooses."

"Well, then, we might as well get it over with," Evan replied. "May my cousins dance the waltz with me?"

Lady Jersey laughed. "I can see you are a man who likes to get right to the point, Lord Althorpe. Yes, your cousins may dance the waltz. But, remember, they must dance their first waltz with *you.*"

Evan grinned at her. "That will be no hardship for me, ma'am. I don't know any of the other young ladies who are here."

"I will present you to some of them," Lady Jersey assured him.

Evan's smile dimmed. "You are very good."

Lady Jersey waved to two young men who had been hovering in our vicinity. "Mr. Singleton, Lord Craig, allow me to introduce you to Miss Lewis and Lady Julia Marshall."

Both gentlemen looked eagerly at Lizzie, and when she smiled at one of them, the other politely turned to me. "Would you care to have this dance with me, Lady Julia?" he asked.

Lord Craig's hair was carefully curled and his necktie came almost up to his ears. I wondered what kind of peripheral vision such a monstrosity would allow. However, not to be outdone in politeness, I produced a smile and said yes, I would dance with him.

The good thing about a minuet is that you don't get a chance to talk very much. The same is true for the cotillion that followed, which I danced with another young man whose name I didn't remember.

The third man I danced with said, as we waited for the set to form, "I was at Tattersall's when your cousin bought that chestnut gelding of Blackburn's. I understand he acquired it for you."

I felt the first spark of interest I had known all evening. "He did buy me a chestnut gelding," I said. "We left my mare at home and I needed something to ride while I was in London."

"I haven't seen you in the park with him yet."

"I've been taking him out early in the morning, so we can gallop. The park in the afternoon is horribly crowded. No fun at all."

He nodded, but before he could reply the music started and the dance began. It was a few minutes before we met up again and when we did, I asked, "I'm curious. Why was he being sold?"

"Blackburn had bought him for his wife, but he was too much horse for her. He's small enough for a woman, but he was bred to be a racehorse. He ran away with her a few times, and that was that."

Once again we were separated by the dance and I looked forward eagerly to reconnecting with this interesting person who knew all about my horse.

"It sounds as if you are doing all right with him," he said to me on our next meeting.

"I love him," I replied fervently. "I think I might try him in the hunting field."

He looked interested. "You hunt, do you?"

"Oh, yes. All the time."

The dance was over, and I stood talking to my partner. For the first time I really looked at him. He was a broad-shouldered young man of average height with brown hair and eyes that were a mix of blue and gray. "What was your name again?" I asked.

He grinned. "I'm Tom Winston. My father is Lord Sheffield. He has a place in Leicestershire, near Melton Mowbray. I hunt with the Quorn myself. But we don't get many ladies."

"I should love to hunt with the Quorn," I said enviously.

"Not too many full-bred Thoroughbreds hunting with the Quorn," Mr. Winston replied. "They're fast, but a little delicate over heavy country. And hard to control sometimes. We mostly use Thoroughbred crosses."

"I've hunted my Thoroughbred mare for years. No other breed has the courage of the Thoroughbred."

Mr. Winston looked at me with respect and I decided that I liked him.

My senses suddenly prickled and I turned to see Evan coming up to me. A waltz was the next dance on the card.

He nodded amiably to Mr. Winston and said to me, "We might as well get this waltz over with. Then you won't have to worry if anyone else asks you."

For some reason, I felt nervous. I wet my lips with my tongue and put my hand into the hand he was holding out to me.

Mr. Winston said, "I say, Lady Julia, would you dance with me again?"

I blinked and looked at him. "Why, yes, I suppose so."

I walked with Evan out to the floor. "That's the first fellow I've seen you talking to," he said.

"Have you been watching me?"

"Just trying to make sure you're getting on all right."

"Oh. He was asking me about Ty," I said. "Just fancy, Evan, he knew all about your outbidding Lord Ormesby. And he knew about Ty's previous owner, too. He was very interesting."

His blue eyes smiled down at me. "I told you to talk about horses."

The music began to play and Evan put his hand on my waist. He was much taller than I, but our steps matched as we began to circle the floor. I felt the movement of his body against mine and suddenly it was as if we were the only two people in the room. We didn't talk. I felt like resting my cheek against his shoulder and dancing with him forever.

When the music stopped I stiffened in surprise. It was an effort for me to step away from him and when I dared to look up into his face, he was staring down at me, his face unsmiling, his eyes narrowed. It was a look that made my breath catch.

What is going on here?

I said, "I think I should go back to Aunt Barbara."

My voice didn't sound quite right.

"I'll take you," he replied. His voice didn't sound quite right either.

I never thought I would be happy to see my aunt, but right now she felt like safety. She gave the two of us an approving smile. "Very nice," she said. "You did me credit, the both of you."

"Thank you," Evan said.

I didn't say anything.

At this point, Lizzie came up with her partner, to whom Aunt Barbara gave an especially gracious smile. "I didn't expect to see *you* here tonight, Your Grace. I thought you were among those who found Almack's unbearably insipid."

The gentleman, who was tall and slim and handsome, with wavy dark brown hair and clear hazel eyes, smiled back. "I was pressed into service by my mother. She has a goddaughter who is making her first appearance tonight and my mother wanted me to escort her."

"Who is she?" Aunt Barbara asked curiously.

He nodded toward a tall, brown-haired girl who was standing across the floor from them. "Miss Hamlin. My mother and hers have been bosom friends for years."

"We're lucky to have my cousin Evan escort us," Lizzie said. "My father hates London. He was thrilled when he heard that he didn't have to come."

The Duke smiled at Evan. "Glad to meet you. It must have felt a little strange to an American, suddenly finding yourself an English earl."

"It feels very strange," Evan replied feelingly.

The music started up and the Duke said to Lizzie, "Thank you for the waltz, Miss Lewis."

I said, "I thought you couldn't dance the waltz until you had danced it with Evan first."

Lizzie laughed. "It seems that dukes have more influence with the patronesses than we do."

Evan said, "I hope that doesn't mean you aren't going to dance with me, Lizzie."

"You shall have the next waltz," she promised.

The duke smiled at me and politely asked me to dance. Politely, I accepted.

*

Going home in the carriage, Aunt Barbara was ecstatic. The Duke of Morton had asked Lizzie to dance twice!

"You must know that he is the biggest catch on the marriage mart, my love," she said. "Has been for years."

"I thought you said Lord Ormesby was the biggest catch," I said.

"Not as big as Morton. A duke! Can you imagine being a duchess, Lizzie?"

"Mama," Lizzie said practically, "he danced with me twice. He didn't propose to me. Calm yourself, please."

"Is a duke more important than an earl?" Evan asked curiously.

"A duke is the highest rank of nobility below the royal family," Lady Barbara said. "Really, Evan, did your father teach you nothing?"

"Americans aren't interested in titles," Evan replied.

"You do have to admit that when the Americans made their revolution, they followed through with it," Lizzie said. "Washington became a president, not a king. The French didn't have as much luck. They ended up with an emperor."

"An excellent point, Lizzie," Evan said warmly.

"I saw you dancing twice with Mr. Winston," Aunt Barbara said to me. "He's not an eligible *parti* for you, Julia. I believe he has a small inheritance from his uncle, but it's not enough to support a wife and family." Her tone of voice was adamant.

"I only danced with him, Aunt Barbara," I said. "He didn't propose."

"I don't know what he was doing at Almack's," she went on with palpable annoyance. "According to Sally Jersey he never comes."

"He came tonight to oblige a friend," I said. "He is up in London looking for a new hunter."

"What kind of a fellow is he?" Evan asked abruptly.

"He hunts with the Quorn!" I said.

"The Quorn is a very famous hunt," Lizzie kindly explained to Evan.

"I'll never understand the fun in galloping across rough country and jumping stone fences, all to catch a little fox," Evan said. "I did it once and that was enough for me."

"And I'll never understand the fun of crossing a huge and dangerous ocean in a little boat!" I shot back.

"I make money doing that," he pointed out. "What money is there in chasing a fox?"

"Money isn't everything in life," I said. "But you Americans don't seem to understand that."

"Listening to Aunt Barbara, it seems to me as if money is pretty important to the English too. At least to the English when they are marrying off their daughters."

A chilly silence fell.

Lizzie, the peacemaker, said, "Let's not quarrel and spoil our lovely evening. You danced with some pretty girls, Evan. Did you have fun?"

"Everyone wants to know about the Red Indians," Evan said. "You would think it wasn't safe to walk the streets of Boston, for God's sake."

"Is it safe?" I asked.

"A lot safer than London," he retorted. "I've never seen such wretched poverty in my life as in this city. Everyone in America who wants a job has one. From what I have observed here, at least half of the people are unemployed, with no chance of getting a job either. So they turn to crime. I'd rather walk down a dark street in Boston than in London any day."

Lizzie said, "Papa says it's getting worse, too. All of the soldiers who fought in the war against Napoleon are coming home, and there's no work for them. And Parliament has passed this Corn Law, to keep the price of corn up so that English farmers can make a profit. But Papa says such a law will hurt the poor badly."

"Your father sounds like a good man, Lizzie," Evan said approvingly.

Aunt Barbara said, "You will have an opportunity to meet my husband when he comes to London for our ball. He's a bit of a radical, I'm afraid. You will probably get along very well."

I said, "I didn't know about this Corn Law. It sounds very stupid to me. If people have to pay more money for bread, they won't have anything left over to buy bacon, cheese, butter, milk, beer, meat—all the other products English farmers produce. That's not only going to hurt the poor, it's going to hurt the farmer in the long run too."

"How clever of you, Julia," Lizzie said. "That's exactly what Papa says."

"Enough of this political talk," Aunt Barbara pronounced. "You girls may sleep late tomorrow morning, but you must be ready to receive visitors by eleven. I am quite certain that a number of gentlemen will be calling."

"I can't sleep late," I said. "I have to take Ty to the park so he can get some exercise."

"Take him out in the afternoon, when the *ton* will be in the park," Aunt Barbara said. "Isn't that why you got him? So you could ride in the park with us?"

"One doesn't *ride* at five o'clock in the park," I said. "There's too much traffic to do more than a sedate trot. It's boring." I turned to Evan. "You won't be too tired to go out tomorrow morning, will you, Evan?"

"Not at all," he said. "I don't mind a good gallop. Just don't ask me to jump any fences."

There was a faint teasing note in his voice, and I felt a tightness inside me, that I hadn't even realized was there, relax.

"I won't," I promised.

"Here we are," said Aunt Barbara, and the coach turned into the courtyard of Althorpe House.

Chapter Twenty-Three

I was tired when I got to bed, but sleep wouldn't come. I kept thinking about that waltz with Evan and the way it made me feel.

Deep in my heart, I knew Evan was the one man I could spend the rest of my life with. If only he would stay in England! We could live at Stoverton and together we would bring it back to life. If only he wasn't an American!

But he was American, and he had made it clear he was returning to America, so that was that. I couldn't turn my back on Stoverton and its people and sail off to America with Evan – even had he wanted me to, which was unlikely. I wasn't a suitable wife for an American who ran a business. Evan needed a sensible girl who would be happy to live in little Salem, where there was no art, no hunting and—from what I gathered—no decent horses. Our plans for the future just did not mesh.

I had barely caught an hour's sleep when I met Evan in the stable to take Ty to the park.

*

After breakfast I dressed in one of my new morning gowns and went downstairs with Lizzie to sit in the drawing room to await callers. I was feeling tired and grumpy and took the seat Aunt Barbara waved me to with ill grace. At precisely eleven o'clock the door knocker sounded and the callers began to arrive.

I was greatly relieved to find that most of them had come for Lizzie. Unfortunately, when they couldn't get close to Lizzie, they felt they had to talk to me. On a good day I would have had a hard time speaking sensibly to men who prattled on about dancing and the weather, and this was not a good day. In fact, I was in a foul mood and it was an effort to get beyond monosyllables.

It was with relief that I saw Mr. Winston come into the room. He went to make his presence known to Aunt Barbara and came directly to sit in the empty seat beside me. The idiot who had been babbling at me had finally given up and taken his leave, thank God.

I gave him a warm smile. "I am so glad to see you, Mr. Winston. Please promise me not to talk about the weather."

He smiled back and held up his hand as if taking an oath. "I promise."

We had a most interesting conversation about hunting. He had some fascinating stories that had me hanging on his every word. It wasn't until the whole room went quiet that we looked away from each other to see what had happened.

The Duke of Morton stood in the doorway. He advanced confidently into the room and greeted Aunt Barbara, who looked like the cat who swallowed the canary. Then he turned toward Lizzie and began to approach her chair. One of the men sitting next to her hastily vacated his place so the ducal bottom could possess it.

I said to Mr. Winston, "My American cousin would be horrified if he saw that little display of aristocratic power."

"I suppose some of our ways must seem strange to him," Mr. Winston said. "It will take him a while to grow accustomed to being an earl."

"I don't think he plans to stay around long enough to grow accustomed," I said.

Mr. Winston looked surprised. "Is he going back to America?"

"That's his plan."

Mr. Winston said, "But what about Stoverton? I understand it needs...er...some attention."

"It needs a great deal of attention," I said baldly. "And money. I believe he plans to make some...arrangements."

He nodded and smiled. "I say, Lady Julia, would you care to come for a ride in the park with me this afternoon?"

I thought this was a wonderful idea. I had galloped Ty hard this morning so he should be well enough behaved this afternoon. We were making plans when Lizzie called my name.

I looked over to where she was sitting with the duke beside her. "Are you planning to go to the park this afternoon?" she asked.

"Yes. Mr. Winston and I were just talking about it."

Lizzie turned to the duke. "Perhaps we could join my cousin and Mr. Winston, Your Grace."

The Duke's handsome face looked perfectly amiable. "That would be delightful."

The calling hour was over and the gentlemen began to get up to leave. When the room was finally empty Aunt Barbara gazed at Lizzie with stars in her eyes. "Morton actually called! And you are going to the park with him this afternoon. Oh, Lizzie! I knew you would make a good match, but a duke!"

Lizzie just smoothed her dress over her lap and didn't answer.

I said, "What if Lizzie doesn't like him? She's not going to marry him just because he's a duke."

Aunt Barbara looked at me as if I were insane. "What is there not to like about Morton? He's handsome, he's only twenty-eight, he has plenty of money, and he's a duke. There is no reason in the world not to like him."

"You have to do more than like a man to marry him, Mama," Lizzie pointed out. "You have to love him."

"Believe me, it's just as easy to love a duke as it is an ordinary man," Aunt Barbara retorted.

Lizzie and I exchanged looks.

Lizzie said, "Mr. Winston seems very nice, Julia."

"I'm curious to see how he looks on a horse," I said.

Lizzie laughed and Aunt Barbara frowned. "I thought I told you Thomas Winston is not a suitable match for you, Julia. I don't want to see you spending time with him. You need to look around for someone who can offer you a home, not a younger son who spends all his money on horses."

In fact, it had occurred to me that Tom Winston was exactly the kind of man Evan had told me to look for. Since he had no estate of his own, he should be happy to come and live at Stoverton. And clearly he liked the country life—he had told me he didn't come to London very often. He sounded almost perfect. And he seemed nice.

It was too bad that the prospect of marrying this perfect man and living with him at Stoverton made me feel so gloomy.

*

Aunt Barbara, Lizzie and I had almost finished luncheon when the dining room door opened and Evan, Maria and Miss Dixon came in. They had color in their cheeks and looked to be in high good humor.

"I hope we're not too late to eat," Evan said to Grantly. "We're starving."

"Of course not, my lord," the butler replied. "I shall bring some more cold meat and bread."

"Thank you," Evan replied. He turned to Maria and her governess. "Sit down, sit down. I'm sure you both want some food."

Maria went with alacrity to take her chair, but Miss Dixon held back a little, looking anxiously at Aunt Barbara.

Aunt Barbara glanced at Evan, then back at the hesitant governess. She nodded briefly and Miss Dixon moved to take a seat.

I looked at her. She was wearing a plain gray gown and her thick auburn hair was pulled back into a severe chignon. Even so, she was an extremely pretty and obviously well-bred young woman. I wondered what had happened to necessitate her earning her own living.

It isn't fair, I thought. If Miss Dixon had been a man she could have gone to India and made a fortune. Men aren't forced to become governesses when they're poor.

"...went to the Tower," Maria was saying, and I pulled my attention back to the conversation.

"You went to the Tower?" I demanded. "Why didn't you tell me? I would have gone with you!"

Evan replied, "You were engaged here this morning, and Maria asked me if I would take her. I must say it was very interesting."

"Evan liked best the place where all those people were beheaded," Maria said teasingly.

"Who was the one who knew all the gory details?" he retorted.

She giggled. "I knew about King Henry's queens. It was Miss Dixon who knew about the others."

"Miss Dixon was a mine of information," Evan said, with a smile at the governess. "Better than a tour guide."

I was irate. I had been forced to sit indoors being polite to strangers while Maria and Evan were having fun at the Tower!

Evan completely ignored my scowl and began to eat the cold meat that had been set upon the table.

Maria said apologetically, "I would have asked you, Julia, but you were busy with company."

Evan said calmly, "Stop sulking, Julia. It doesn't become you."

Everyone around the table stopped breathing.

I narrowed my eyes. "When you made me come to London, you said that you would take me to see the sights. I distinctly recall that discussion. And then, the first place you visit, you leave me behind!"

We stared at each other.

Still nobody breathed.

He said, "As I believe I've told you before, I always keep my promises. I'll take you and Lizzie to the Tower another day, when you are not engaged."

"And you said we would go to Astley's!"

"We will go to Astley's when it is convenient for Aunt Barbara to let you go."

I turned to Aunt Barbara, my eyes narrowed, daring her to deny me. Evan said mildly, "When do we have a free afternoon, ma'am?"

"I believe tomorrow would be acceptable," she said, looking down her nose at me.

"Very well. I will get tickets for tomorrow."

"Thank you," I replied, a little haughtily. I was still annoyed that he had gone to the Tower without me.

Evan turned to the governess. "Would you care to join us, Miss Dixon?"

"That won't be necessary, Evan," Aunt Barbara said. "I'm sure Miss Dixon can find something to do at home."

Miss Dixon's eyelids flickered but otherwise her expression didn't change.

Poor girl, I thought. How rotten to be treated like a servant.

I said, "There's nothing Miss Dixon has to do that can't be done some other time, Aunt Barbara." I turned to the governess. "Do come. It will be fun."

Before the governess could answer, Evan said, "That's settled, then. I'll get the tickets." His eyes caught mine for a brief second before he said gravely, "Would you care to come with us, Aunt Barbara?"

My aunt was so stunned she couldn't immediately answer. Finally she managed, "No, Evan, I do not wish to go to Astleys."

She said the word as if it were Hades.

I had to bite my lip to keep from smiling.

"Then that is settled," Evan said. He turned to Lizzie, "What are you doing this afternoon?"

"Julia and I are going for a ride in the park with the Duke of Morton and Mr. Winston," she replied.

Evan said to me, "You're taking Ty into the park with all that traffic? He's not ready for that. You could get hurt."

I ignored the blue glare that was directed at my face. "We galloped hard this morning. He'll be too tired to act up. It will be fine."

The blue glare didn't change.

Aunt Barbara said, "I do hope you are not going to fall off and make a spectacle of yourself, Julia. That would be most embarrassing."

"I never fall off," I said. This was not true, of course. No one could ride for as long as I had and never fall off. But I was quite confident that I would not fall off Ty in the park. He might rear a little…buck a little…but I would not fall off.

Evan wisely changed the subject, "Julia and I saw that Byron fellow as we were coming home from our ride this morning. I guess they've finally moved in across the street."

"You saw Lord Byron?" Miss Dixon said, surprised into speech.

Lizzie turned to her. "Yes, he's taken the house across the street. Isn't that exciting? Have you read his poetry, Miss Dixon?"

"I have." The governess' face was bright with enthusiasm.

"'The Corsair,'" Lizzie said, clasping her hands dramatically at her breast.

"Wonderful," Miss Dixon enthused.

Evan and I looked at each other. *Terrible poetry* I mouthed at him.

He nodded in agreement.

"Enough of Lord Byron," Aunt Barbara said. "I think I have found a music teacher for Maria. His name is Heinrich Gruder. He was a pianist attached to the court of one of the German states – I forget which one at the moment. He's been in London for a few years now and he will take a student if the student has enough talent. He is coming later this afternoon to hear Maria play."

Maria looked even more enraptured at this announcement than Lizzie and Miss Dixon had looked about Lord Byron.

"Oh Aunt Barbara, thank you!" A little of her joy dimmed. "But...what if I'm not good enough for him?"

"Just play your best," Aunt Barbara replied briskly. "You are very good, Maria. You must know that yourself."

When Maria didn't answer I put in, "Of course she knows it. We all know it. This German pianist will love you."

"Aunt Barbara is right," Evan said. "Just play your best. And if this fellow doesn't want to teach you, we'll find someone else who will."

Maria's radiance returned. "All right." She looked at her aunt. "If you don't mind, Aunt Barbara, I will go practice."

Lady Barbara smiled her acquiescence.

Miss Dixon also stood. "I will go upstairs and finish tidying up the schoolroom."

"I'll come with you," I said. "We can take inventory of what books are there and you can tell me what else you think you need."

"That would be very kind of you, Lady Julia," the governess said in her soft pretty voice.

"Don't forget we're going to the park at five," Lizzie said.

"I won't," I promised as I left the dining room with Miss Dixon.

Chapter Twenty-Four

Evan spent the afternoon with the American Minister discussing America's future. John Quincy Adams' vision for the United States was ambitious and visionary. He saw it stretching all the way south into Florida (presently owned by Spain), then west, through the Rocky Mountains and on into California (also owned by Spain). From ocean to ocean the nation would grow, he prophesied grandly.

It was a heroic dream, and a dream Evan thought was attainable. After all, the United States had already doubled its size by Jefferson's purchase of the Louisiana territory from France.

Although Evan agreed with the minister, he did his best during their time together to suggest tactfully that perhaps it would be best for Mr. Adams not to share this glorious vision with the English government just yet.

When Evan returned to Althorpe House, Julia and Lizzie had just come in from their afternoon ride. He scanned Julia from head to toe and demanded, "Did Ty behave himself?"

"He was fine,"" she said airily. "A little skittish on the way to the park perhaps, but once we got there he behaved himself admirably."

Evan turned to Lizzie for confirmation. She assured him, "I wouldn't ride Ty for a million guineas, but Julia handles him beautifully. He really is a lovely horse. Everyone was looking at us."

"He's gorgeous," Julia said complacently. "He moves like an angel."

"Well, I'm glad it went well," Evan said.

"It was a successful afternoon. Julia even approved of Mr. Winston's horsemanship," Lizzie said with a laugh.

"Oh?" said Evan, uncomfortably conscious of his own failure in that department.

"Yes," Julia said. "He has perfect balance in the saddle. He was riding a borrowed horse because his own horses are back in Leicestershire, but even on an inferior animal I could see how well he rode."

"That's nice," Evan said woodenly.

Julia shot him a look, then said to Lizzie, "Ty is marvelous, but I think the reason people were looking at us was because you were riding with the Duke."

"I guess this Duke really is a big deal," Evan said. "What do you make of him, Lizzie?"

"He's nice," Lizzie returned.

"He liked Ty," Julia said, offering her stamp of approval.

It was such a Julia remark that Evan and Lizzie both smiled.

Evan surveyed them both. "Well, you look very nice in your new riding clothes."

"I hate breaking in new boots," Julia said gloomily. "I wish Aunt Barbara had let me keep my old ones."

"You're not the only one who feels like that," Evan returned. "This coat is too tight across my shoulders and this neck cloth is so starched it scratches my skin."

"But you look splendid, Evan," Lizzie said. "At Almack's you were by far the most handsome man in the room."

"That is kind of you, Lizzie," he said with faint amusement.

"You were," Julia put in. When he looked at her in surprise she added, "You're the image of the first earl, and he was considered the most handsome man of his day."

"Do you know, Julia, I'm getting rather tired of being compared to the first earl." Even Evan could hear the irritation in his voice.

She looked bewildered. "But I meant it as a compliment!"

He looked back at her and the only thought in his mind was how beautiful she was. He supposed, objectively, Lizzie's face was more perfect, but for him Julia's face, with its amazing gray eyes, delicate bones, and look of flawless pride was heart stirring.

He tried to think of something commonplace to say but nothing came to mind. Then the sound of a piano came from the back of the house.

"Do you know how Maria's meeting with Herr Gruder went?" he asked Lizzie.

"No. Let's find out."

The three of them walked down the hall to the drawing room, where Maria was alone at the piano. She was so absorbed in her music that she didn't hear them until Julia called her name. Then she swung around on her chair, showing them a smiling face.

Evan felt a surge of happiness. He had grown very fond of this young cousin. "So, he's going to take you on," he said.

"Yes." Maria clasped her hands in front of her. "Oh, Evan, he said I was very talented!"

"Well, we all knew that," Julia said.

"That's wonderful," Evan said.

"I'm so happy for you, Maria," Lizzie said.

"I'm afraid he's going to be very expensive, Evan." Maria looked at him worriedly. "Much more expensive than an ordinary music teacher."

"Don't worry about the expense," Evan assured her. "Julia keeps telling me that there's more to life than money, and in this case, she's right. God has given you a great gift and you should cultivate it. It makes me happy to help you."

Julia turned a glowing face up to him. His breath caught and hot desire ran through him like a bolt of lightning. He had to look away so she wouldn't see it.

"Thank you, Evan." She cleared her throat and went on, her words sounding as if she had practiced them, "I'm sorry I was so unpleasant to you when you first arrived. I didn't give you a chance and…I apologize. It was not well done of me."

Evan also took a deep breath and managed to look at her again. "Apology accepted," he said huskily.

*

The come-out ball for Julia and Lizzie was a week away and Lady Barbara was so busy with her plans that the young people in the household found themselves with more unscheduled time than usual. Evan, who vividly remembered Julia's disappointed face when she learned he had gone to the Tower without her, took her one morning. They went by themselves as Lizzie and Maria had other plans.

They spent an enjoyable morning together. Even though Julia had never been to the Tower, she knew even more about it than Miss Dixon had. She and Evan soon collected a group of school children who followed them around listening to Julia's every word. Not wanting to disappoint her audience, Julia made her narrative as gory as possible. The children loved it. So did Evan.

On their way home Evan suggested they stop at Gunter's for an ice cream. Julia was in enthusiastic agreement. As they sat at a table spooning up the delicious pistachio ice cream they had ordered, Evan brought up the subject of possible suitors.

"You seem to like this Winston fellow," he remarked as offhandedly as he could manage.

"Tom is a great gun," she replied, licking her lip to get the last taste of ice cream. Evan quickly looked away. "We have a lot in common. There's always something interesting for us to talk about."

"I know that Aunt Barbara has been telling you Winston is not an eligible parti, but you do know, Julia, that your husband doesn't need to have money. I will always take care of you."

She put down her spoon and kept her eyes on it. Her lashes were so long they almost touched her cheek. She said, "Actually, Aunt Barbara is wrong about Tom. He told me he has a nice inheritance from an uncle, so he's not poor at all."

164

Evan knew he should be happy to hear this. Julia had found the perfect man – the very type of man he had encouraged her to look for. Tom (he hated it that she was now calling him 'Tom') Winston was a younger son, with money, who would probably be happy to help Julia with her restoration projects at Stoverton. They could hunt together, and she could have as many horses as she wanted. Her life would be exactly what she wanted it to be.

Julia looked up at him and smiled. "When can we go to the theatre?"

"Do you want to see this Kean fellow in the Merchant of Venice?"

"Yes, I do."

"I'll see about getting tickets then."

"Do you know, London wouldn't be a bad place to visit, if only one didn't have to keep going to parties."

"Come along," he said, "we've kept the horses waiting long enough."

Chapter Twenty-Five

Two days before the come-out ball Evan came into the upstairs living room to find Lady Barbara, Lizzie, Julia and Maria seated around a man Evan had never seen before. Lady Barbara quickly introduced her husband and Evan went to shake his hand.

Gordon Lewis was a handsome man in his fifties, with graying blonde hair and dark blue eyes. He rose from his seat to take Evan's hand into a strong grip. "You've done me a great favor by taking on the escort duties for my wife and daughter. Not to mention allowing us to use your house. I greatly appreciate it, Althorpe." He glanced at his wife and admitted, "I have little patience for this kind of thing."

Evan said wryly, "It's not my kind of thing, either, but I got pressed into service. It's nice to have another man in the house."

Gordon gave him a commiserating look and Evan thought he was going to like Lizzie's father.

At dinner Lady Barbara talked about the upcoming ball. Evan, listening politely to his aunt's monologue, caught Julia's eye across the table. She rolled her eyes and he tried to suppress a grin.

When merciful silence descended on Lady Barbara, Maria turned to Evan, "Miss Dixon doesn't have anything appropriate to wear to the ball, Evan." She was looking at him expectantly, clearly anticipating he would do something to rectify this problem.

Before he could answer, however, the governess said hastily, "I am not going to the ball, Maria, so I have no need of a dress." She conjured up a tense smile. "You and I can have a special supper in the schoolroom."

"A very good idea," Lady Barbara said approvingly.

"Of course Miss Dixon is coming to the ball," Evan said to his aunt. "I invited her myself."

Everyone looked at Miss Dixon, whose cheeks had flushed a deep pink, making her look even prettier than usual. "I told you, my lord, that it would not be appropriate for me to attend such a function. It is kind enough that you allow me to dine with the family, but I cannot attend your ball."

"But of course you can!" said the warm-hearted Lizzie. "You are prettier than most of the ladies who will be attending, and I have a gown that will look lovely on you."

Miss Dixon shook her head, looking at Lady Barbara, anxiety writ clear on her face.

Gordon Lewis said, "My daughter is right. Of course you must come. I'm sure Lizzie will be happy to introduce you to some young men." He looked at his wife. "She seems a very well-bred young lady, my dear."

To Evan's astonishment, Lady Barbara's face relaxed. "Of course she is well-bred, Gordon. I wouldn't have hired her for Maria if she wasn't."

And the question of Miss Dixon's presence at the ball was settled.

*

When dinner was finished Gordon indicated he would like a glass of port, and Evan, as host, remained at the table with him while the ladies retired. The two men talked for a while on general subjects and the picture Evan got of Lizzie's father was that of an intelligent, thoughtful, well-read man, who was happy living quietly in the country. He sounded as if he was a good landlord and a good local magistrate.

"You're doing a fine thing for Julia, giving her this season," Gordon said as they started on their second glass of port. "Althorpe was a bounder—and an inept bounder at that. He was a bad husband, a bad father, a bad landowner and an inveterate gambler. He was also a coward who left his daughters to face the consequences of his own reprehensible behavior." He shook his head disgustedly. "My wife tried to get the girls to come and live with us, but Julia wouldn't have it."

"So I've heard."

"She's a handful, eh?"

Evan didn't like hearing Julia described this way. "She kept Stoverton going for years," he said.

"True, true." Gordon put down his glass. "By the way, I want you to understand that I am perfectly prepared to shoulder my half of the cost of this season. I know from past experience that it is outrageously expensive. I appreciate your letting my wife and daughter use your house, but I will not allow you to bear the entire financial burden. You have staff to pay, food to order, and—of course—this damned come-out ball. Divide your bills in two and I'll pay half."

Evan looked at his uncle-by-marriage with approval. This was a man he could respect. Like Evan, he understood that you shouldn't get something for nothing.

"Thank you," he said. "I will be happy to do that."

Gordon's mouth quirked in a smile. "I was afraid you might have heard a different tune from my wife. She still considers herself a Marshall and therefore entitled to Marshall benefits."

Evan laughed.

They finished their port and went to join the ladies in the drawing room.

*

The following morning Julia, Lizzie and Evan drove to the Duke of Morton's home to view his art collection. Julia was excited, Lizzie was her usual even-tempered self, and Evan was resolved not to betray his ignorance.

The duke's collection was extensive, and Evan was more fascinated by the rapt expression on Julia's face then he was by the paintings. He listened to the duke's commentary and tried without success to see in them what Julia was seeing.

There was so much he didn't know. He didn't like this feeling, but he knew it was true. There was something about these pictures he was missing, and he couldn't seem to figure out how to find it.

Finally the duke stopped in front of a painting that took Evan's breath away. Morton said, "I just bought this. It was done by a young English painter whose work I like very much. His name is Turner."

The painting depicted a ship at sea, but the ship was not what drew Evan's attention. What made his breath catch was the immensity of the painted sky and the way it was suffused in radiant, shimmering light. Racing storm clouds, the kind that Evan knew well from personal experience, were scattered across the glowing expanse of the heavens.

"This is wonderful," he said reverently. "This is something you would never tire of looking at."

"Yes," Morton returned. "And Turner is young; he's only going to get better."

Evan turned to the duke. "Does he have any more paintings for sale?"

Morton smiled. "Artists always have paintings for sale, Althorpe. I'll give you his direction."

"Thank you," Evan said with real gratitude. A painting like that would probably be expensive, but it would be something he would look at and enjoy every day of his life. Perhaps he would buy two.

He glanced down at Julia and found her looking at him with smug approval.

She thinks she's converting me, he thought. He looked again at the light-filled painting on the Duke's wall and had to admit that there was something to be said for a civilization that could produce and value a work of art like this painting, which existed not to be useful, but merely to be beautiful.

Once the tour was over, the Duke invited them to stay for tea. Evan was sitting in a Chippendale chair under a huge Renaissance painting of some saint or other, when a slight young man with light brown hair and spectacles came into the room.

"Hallo Roger," the Duke said amiably. "Finally got your nose out of a book? Come and be introduced."

As the young man advanced into the room the light from the window reflected off his spectacles. "Allow me to introduce my brother, Lord Roger Hampton," the Duke said. "Roger, this is Lady Julia, Miss Lewis and Lord Althorpe."

Lord Roger favored them with a sweet, shy smile and shook hands all around. He did not look at all like his handsome, confident brother, Evan thought. But his handshake was firm and his gray eyes held Evan's steadily as he greeted him. He seated himself on the sofa next to Lizzie and accepted a cup of tea.

"Roger has just finished at Oxford, where he won all the prizes," the Duke said. "He is the brains in our family."

Lizzie gave the young man a friendly smile. "What are your plans, now that you have finished school, Lord Roger?"

"I am to be vicar of our parish church at Morton," Roger returned.

Evan looked at the young man in surprise. "Aren't you a little young for such a position?"

"I have complete faith in Roger," the Duke said. He regarded his brother affectionately. "I believe I made a fine choice; he will fill the position admirably."

"I will do my best," Roger replied.

Evan gave Julia a puzzled look and she interpreted it correctly. "In England it is not only the archbishop who has the gift of a parish in his keeping. Many large landowners may appoint the clergy of a parish that is in what we call their 'living.' The Duke has given the living at Morton to his brother."

"I see," Evan said. Privately he thought it sounded a rum thing, for church positions to be in the keeping of private parties. But he smiled at the Duke. "I often need to have things explained to me. We do things differently in America than you do over here."

"That is only natural," the Duke said graciously.

"Are you in London for long, Lord Roger?" Julia asked pleasantly.

"For a month or so. My tenure doesn't start until June."

"Would you like to come to our ball?" Lizzie asked. "It's tomorrow and we would love to have you."

Lord Roger first looked surprised, then uncertain. He turned to his brother.

The Duke said humorously, "Roger has spent so many years with his books, that I don't know if he knows what to do at a ball."

Evan and Julia exchanged amused glances and she said, "We can give you the name of a very good dance instructor, Lord Roger."

Lizzie laughed. "Mr. Martelli. What fun we had with him."

"I know how to dance," Lord Roger said gravely. "My mother insisted that I learn."

Julia said, "Then you must come to our ball. You can dance with me and save me from partners like Mr. Bellford."

"Mr. Bellford?" the duke said. "What is wrong with Bellford, Lady Julia?"

"Everything, according to Julia," Evan said with amusement.

The Duke raised an eyebrow. "He is considered very good *ton*, you know. And he's quite well off."

"He's stupid," Julia replied.

The Duke looked a little startled by this blanket condemnation.

Lizzie said cheerfully, "Lord Roger can't be stupid if he took all the prizes at Oxford."

"My brother exaggerates," Lord Roger said quickly. "I certainly did not take all the prizes."

"Oh? And what one did you miss?" the Duke put in.

Lord Roger gave his shy, sweet smile to Julia. "I would be happy to come to your ball and dance with you, Lady Julia."

"You can dance with me too," Lizzie said.

"You had better sign up now," the Duke advised. "Miss Lewis's dance card fills up as soon as she walks in the door."

Lizzie laughed and shook her head. "As you just pointed out, your brother exaggerates," she said to Lord Roger.

He grinned.

"Actually, he doesn't," Julia said. "There's a stampede every time Lizzie enters a room."

"You don't do too badly yourself," Lizzie retorted.

"Yes, but I get people like Mr. Bellford. I had to waltz with him and do you know what he talked about? His roses! For the entire dance I had to hear about his roses. I had to force myself not to yawn."

The Duke grinned, and for the first time there was a resemblance to his brother. "Don't you like roses, Lady Julia?"

"Of course I like roses. I like to look at roses. I like to smell them. I don't like to hear about planting them and fertilizing them and whatever else one has to do to make them grow."

Lizzie said, "Did it ever occur to you, Julia, that you go on about horses the same way Bellford goes on about roses?

Do you know how many hours I have spent listening to you carry on about how wonderful Ty is?"

Julia looked dumbfounded. "How can you compare a horse to a flower, Lizzie? Horses are living breathing creatures with minds of their own. They're interesting. Roses are just...plants."

Evan looked down at his knees and tried not to laugh.

Lord Roger said gently, "We all have our own passions, Lady Julia. In the interest of human harmony, it is probably best to try to be tolerant of each other."

Julia looked skeptical but didn't reply.

Lizzie said, "Lord Roger is right. Life is more pleasant when people are kind to each other."

"I wasn't unkind to Mr. Bellford," Julia protested. "I didn't yawn."

This time Evan laughed out loud.

The Duke put an end to the conversation by asking Lizzie to put him and his brother down for two dances each. "And I would appreciate it if you would do the same, Lady Julia," he said. "I promise you neither Roger nor I will talk about plants."

"Good," Julia said firmly. "We can talk about horses instead."

Chapter Twenty-Six

The day of the come-out ball dawned with fog and rain. At breakfast it was clear that my aunt was taking the weather as a personal insult.

"My dear, this *is* England," Uncle Gordon said mildly. "The ball is not being held outdoors. Your guests won't melt walking from their carriages to the house. Don't get yourself into a tizzy over nothing."

Aunt Barbara looked at her husband and slowly her exasperation seemed to drain away. "You're right," she said. "There are too many other important things to worry about. And it might clear by evening."

A few days ago I would have been surprised to see my aunt react in so positive a fashion to anyone who admonished her. But, as I had seen them together, I realized that Aunt Barbara respected and cared for her husband. My aunt was a much easier person to deal with when Gordon Lewis was around.

Watching Lizzie with her father mesmerized me. They so clearly loved each other. Seeing them together made me think of my own father, who had been everything my uncle was not. My father hadn't cared one jot for his children. All he had wanted to do was squander away the family fortune on horse racing and games of chance. The last time I had seen him alive was a year after my mother's funeral, when he had come to Stoverton to tell me he had to cut my allowance to run the house.

Lady Barbara's prayers were answered, and the rain let up by nightfall. The dinner guests didn't need umbrellas as they crossed the glistening pavement to the front door of Althorpe House, which was held open by a splendidly liveried footman.

A select group of twenty had been invited to dine, and I was placed between the Marquis of Ormesby and an army officer who introduced himself as Lizzie's cousin. The Marquis was one of the men who regularly asked me to dance, and I knew my aunt was hoping he would make me an offer.

The Marquis would never do for me, of course. He had his own great estate and wouldn't want to spend all his time at Stoverton. Of course, I couldn't say such a thing to Aunt Barbara, nor did I think the Marquis was about to propose, so I did my best to be pleasant to him. He owned some racehorses, which made conversation fairly easy.

Lizzie and I wore fancier dresses than we had worn to previous balls. These dresses featured a new style according to the dressmaker. They had a decorative underskirt, which was worn under a partially open dress of worked French muslin. Frankly, I liked the simpler ones we had worn to the earlier balls better. But then, as Aunt Barbara had said when I shared this remark with her, what did I know about fashion?

My gown was an unusual shade—a pale gray French muslin. Aunt Barbara had been outraged by the dressmaker's suggestion of gray, which was a mourning color, but when she had seen the fabric, which almost exactly matched my eyes, she had agreed to it. Lizzie's abigail had dressed my hair in an elegant knot high on the back of my head. The fashion was for short hair with curls around the face, but my hair didn't curl, and I refused to sit for an hour while someone fussed over it.

I looked quite nice, if I do say so myself. Evan had even looked at me before looking at Lizzie, who, as always, looked like a goddess.

When we were all seated at table and the soup was being served, I sneaked a glance at Evan, who was sitting in the host's position at one end of the long table opposite Aunt Barbara. He looked so splendid in his black evening coat. Both a Duke and a Marquis graced our table, but Evan outshone them both.

He is everything one could wish for in an Earl of Althorpe, I thought. I wish he'd stay in England! Then perhaps we could…

As soon as I realized what I was thinking, I pulled myself up short. This won't do! I scolded myself. Our futures were plain: Evan would go home and marry some boring American girl and I would marry Tom Winston.

I had decided Tom would make a good husband. He had grown up on a large estate and knew what the upkeep entailed. He loved country life. He hunted with the Quorn and had promised to see if he could persuade the Master to let me ride out with them. And I liked him. There was an easiness between us, a familiarity I felt with no other man I had met in London.

But Tom wasn't big and blond, and when we danced I didn't feel as if his body enclosed mine so that my heart quickened and my blood ran hot.

"What do you think of that, Lady Julia?"

It was the Marquis, the dinner companion with whom I was required to make conversation. I turned to him and said, "I'm sorry. I wasn't following. Would you mind repeating that?"

*

The flow of guests kept Aunt Barbara, Uncle Gordon, Evan, Lizzie and me standing at the top of the stairs for an hour before we could enter the ballroom. Finally we went inside, where we opened the ball, Evan dancing with Lizzie and me dancing with Uncle Gordon.

After that, the night proceeded as so many had before it. I danced with the Marquis. I danced with Tom. I danced with a few other men, then with Tom again. We were standing together at the side of the dance floor when I saw Miss Dixon slip in.

I knew she was nervous about coming into such grand company and she looked very alone as she stood near the wall watching the next dance form up on the floor.

"Come along," I said to Tom. "We need to rescue Miss Dixon."

"Who's Miss Dixon?" he asked as he followed me.

"Maria's governess. She's a very nice young woman and we have to make certain she has someone to dance with."

"Is that she? The one against the wall?"

"Yes."

"I'll dance with her," Tom said. "She looks pretty."

In fact, Miss Dixon looked beautiful. She was tall and slim and Lizzie's pale gold dress looked lovely with her auburn hair.

We came up to her and I presented Tom, who promptly asked her to dance. A faint flush stained her porcelain cheeks as she looked at me.

"He thinks you're pretty," I said.

"I most certainly do," Tom agreed.

Miss Dixon's flush grew brighter, but she put her hand in Tom's and let him walk her to the floor.

I was smiling like the cat that ate the cream when Evan came up behind me.

"Thank you, Julia. I've been watching for her, but you got to her first."

I looked up at him. He was watching Tom and Miss Dixon move together as the dance started.

"She's very pretty," I said.

"She's lovely," he replied, emphasizing the *lovely*. "I'll never understand why a beautiful, intelligent young woman like that is not accepted into society."

He thought Miss Dixon was lovely. Beautiful. Intelligent. I knew he would apply none of these encomiums to me. I immediately felt depressed.

"She has no money," I said, "and her father was a vicar of decent but modest birth."

"She should come to America," Evan said. "The men would be fighting to marry a girl like that."

I felt as if a sword had pierced my heart. He was in love with Miss Dixon!

I made myself say, "Why don't you marry her?"

He looked astonished. "I have no intention of marrying Miss Dixon. I merely said that she would find plenty of suitors in America."

The sword disappeared and I smiled as if he had given me a trunkful of gold. "Good," I said. "I don't think you two would suit."

At this point the horrid Mr. Bellford appeared in front of me. "I believe mine is the next dance, Lady Julia."

I gave Evan a meaningful stare, but he only looked as if he were trying not to laugh and said nothing.

I said, "I am so sorry, Mr. Bellford, but my cousin has just asked for this dance and I cannot refuse him. Why don't you come back later?"

"But this is *my* dance, Lady Julia!" Mr. Bellford was clearly put out.

"Mr. Bellford is right, Julia," Evan said. "I wouldn't want to steal his dance. I see that Miss Dixon is free. I'll go and ask her."

He bestowed a bow upon Bellford and a humorous look on me, and left me to the mercy of that man and his bloody roses.

*

The ball had been underway for some time when the Duke of Morton's brother appeared at the doorway. Lord Roger was dressed in the correct attire and his hair had been properly cut, but he looked very young as he regarded the dancing crowd in front of him. I was just about to drag my partner across the floor so I could greet him when I saw Lizzie had got there before me.

I saw Lord Roger give her a grateful smile. The music started and I looked to see who Lizzie was supposed to be dancing with. It was the Marquis, and he didn't look happy about being left on the dance floor by himself.

Aunt Barbara will murder Lizzie, I thought as the dance began and my partner and I paraded down the middle of the floor. At least it wasn't the Duke she dumped.

It was too late for Lizzie and Lord Roger to join the dance, so I expected she would introduce the Duke's brother to some nice girls. However, when I looked around for her when the dance was over, she wasn't there. Nor was Lord Roger.

I peered across the floor at Aunt Barbara, who looked like thunder. Tom appeared beside me and asked if I'd like to go outside on the balcony for a breath of air.

Since I had no recollection of the man who was supposed to get this next dance, I consigned him to perdition and agreed. We stepped out the French doors onto the long, narrow balcony and discovered that two other people had got there before us.

Lizzie and Lord Roger.

Lizzie gave me a dazzling smile. "Were you finding the ballroom too warm as well, Julia?"

"Yes." I looked at Lord Roger, sending him a message with my eyes. He said in his soft, gentle voice, "Perhaps I have kept you out here too long, Miss Lewis. Your mother will be looking for you."

"She is." I sent the same message to Lizzie as I had to Lord Roger: Get back into the ballroom. Now.

I had a brilliant inspiration. "Why don't you introduce Lord Roger to Miss Dixon?" I said to Lizzie.

She narrowed her eyes. Lizzie actually narrowed her eyes.

What is going on here? I thought.

"Perhaps," she said shortly.

After the two of them left, Tom and I looked at each other. "Isn't that Morton's younger brother?" he asked.

"Yes, it is."

"Have he and Miss Lewis met before this?"

"Once."

"Hmm. Not very wise of her to disappear out on the balcony with him like that."

"People might say the same thing of us,' I retorted. I felt I should protect Lizzie.

He grinned at me. He had a lovely smile. He picked up my hand and kissed it. I really liked him very much.

The balcony door opened and Evan came out. Tom dropped my hand and the two of us looked at him like a *guilty thing surprised,* as Hamlet would put it.

Evan looked grim. "I think you should come back into the ballroom, Julia. The Marquis was looking for you."

Tom said hastily, "We just came out for a breath of air, my lord. We're going in right now."

He took my arm and steered me toward the door. I had to pass Evan on the narrow balcony and, as I went by him, I stepped on his toe. Hard.

He swore.

I smiled up at him. "I'm so sorry, my lord. There' just not room out here for so many people."

I went back inside and had my dance with the Marquis.

Chapter Twenty-Seven

The morning after the ball, when a sleep-deprived Evan came downstairs, a footman told him that Sir Gordon and Lady Lewis wished to see him in the library.

"Now?" Evan asked doubtfully. He badly needed a cup of tea.

"Yes, my lord. Lady Barbara has a tea tray in the library."

Evan made his way down the passage, a slight frown between his thick, blond brows. What could be on Aunt Barbara's mind that she should demand to see him so early in the day? After last night's ball he had expected her to remain in bed for most of the morning.

He opened the door and saw his aunt and uncle sitting near the fireplace drinking tea. A small rosewood table had been drawn up in front of Lady Barbara with a teapot and a tray of toast and muffins resting on its polished surface.

"Come in, Evan," she said. "I'm sorry to take you away from your breakfast but there is tea here if you want some."

He sat in a chair close to them and took the cup she handed him. After he had drained the cup and felt the hot liquid wake up his brain, he said, "What is so urgent that you must see me before breakfast?"

There was a short silence while Lady Barbara looked at her husband. He sighed and put down his cup. "We may have a problem, Evan, concerning Julia."

"Julia?" He looked from one face to the other. "I thought she was behaving extremely well."

"Her behavior is not the issue," Lady Barbara said. "The problem is that she appears to have developed a partiality for Thomas Winston, and he for her. Julia cannot be allowed to marry Thomas Winston, Evan. Such a union is unthinkable."

"Really?" Evan's spirits rose. He knew there was something not right about the fellow. "Why?"

Silence fell as Lady Barbara looked at her husband once again. Sir Gordon spoke, "She cannot marry him because he is her half-brother."

It was a good thing the teacup was no longer in Evan's hand or he would have dropped it. He shook his head as if he hadn't heard right. "I beg your pardon, sir, but how can that be?"

"It's simple enough." Lady Barbara took over, her voice very clipped. "Julia's mother, Helen, was the Earl of Sheffield's mistress for years. It is Sheffield who is Julia's father, not Philip. As he is also Thomas Winston's father, you can see the problem that faces us."

Evan was too stunned to speak. His brain balked at what he had just heard. Julia was not his uncle's daughter?

"How can you be sure who her father is?" he finally asked, his voice hoarse.

"The timing. Philip was in London and Helen was visiting an assortment of country houses during the time Julia was conceived."

"They may have got together for a night or two," Evan protested.

Lady Barbara shook her head. "You may have noticed that Julia doesn't look like us. However, she looks very like the Earl of Sheffield. Those eyes."

"Then my uncle must have known. But...he accepted Julia into the family as if she was his."

"He had no choice. I realize Evan that you may be naïve about such things, but in our world Helen played the game properly. She and Sheffield were discreet; they never flaunted their liaison. And she had already provided Althorpe with two healthy sons. She had done her duty by him and she was entitled to lead her own life. Not even I could blame her; Philip was such a chuckle-head."

Evan was speechless. He didn't know what shocked him more, Julia's mother's unfaithfulness or his aunt's easy acceptance of it.

"Does this sort of thing happen frequently in 'your world,' Aunt?"

"You are shocked. But when two people marry for property or dynastic advantage it only seems reasonable to allow them to pursue a love life somewhere else. Once an heir has been produced, of course."

Evan looked at his uncle, who smiled wryly. "One of the reasons I am happiest in the country, my boy." He put his hand over his wife's. "I am in the fortunate position of having a wife who is loyal to me."

Lady Barbara smiled at her husband, then turned back to Evan. "So you see why we cannot allow Julia to develop a *tendre* for Thomas Winston. A marriage between them is impossible."

Evan stared at the teapot and wished it contained brandy. "Julia knows nothing of this?"

Sir Gordon said, "Of course not. Who would tell her such a thing?"

Evan got up and went to the small cabinet in the corner of the library where the brandy was kept. He poured himself a liberal amount, brought it back to his chair and took a big swallow. Then he said, "What about Maria? She certainly looks like a Marshall."

His aunt and uncle exchanged another glance. Evan finished the brandy and said, "Tell me."

"There was an extremely handsome Russian diplomat in London for a brief assignment. Blond haired and blue-eyed. He was also a very fine musician. He played the violin.

Evan slumped forward, his face in his hands.

Sir Gordon said, "I am sorry you had to hear this, Evan. I hope this doesn't change your sense of responsibility for your cousins. They are not responsible for their birth and they are alone in the world."

But they're not my cousins, Evan thought. His head jerked up as another thought hit him. *Julia's not my cousin after all!*

He realized that his aunt and uncle were looking at him with apprehension and he said, "Of course I am still responsible for Julia and Maria. This information doesn't change that."

His aunt rewarded him with a relieved smile. "I knew we could count on you."

Evan frowned. Why had his aunt and uncle brought him into this? Surely they could have handled the situation without his having to know—although it had turned out to be information he found surprisingly welcome.

"But what do you want *me* to do, ma'am?"

"Drive to Sheffield Court and tell the earl he must call his son home from London immediately. Once Thomas is removed from the scene, Julia will have to find someone else. I actually have hopes of Ormesby. He seems to like her company. Imagine if Julia, of all people, became a Marchioness!"

She would hate it, Evan thought.

Sir Gordon said, "There is no reason for the girls to know about this. By law they are the children of the Earl of Althorpe and nothing can take that away from them. They are Marshalls. Period."

But Julia isn't a Marshall, Evan thought. What would she do if she found out the truth? Her whole identity was based on the fact she was a Marshall. Her pride in her family's history, her pride in Stoverton, all of that would be taken away if she found out. A cold chill ran up and down Evan's spine. He must do everything he could to keep this secret.

"Why do you want me to drive to Sheffield?" he asked. "Wouldn't it be more discreet to send a letter?"

Sir Gordon said, "Letters can get misplaced; I don't want to entrust information like this to a letter. I would go but this request should properly come from the person who is responsible for Julia. And that, my boy, is you."

"All right," Evan said. "I'll go today. The sooner we are rid of Winston the better."

186

"Excellent. Sheffield Court is in Kent, not far from Stoverton. If you want, you can be back in London by evening."

Evan stood and felt the brandy on his empty stomach shoot to his head. "I'll breakfast first and then be on my way. What will you tell the girls when they see I'm gone?"

"We'll tell them you went to Stoverton to get some papers for the bank loan," Sir Gordon said.

"Very well." Evan frowned and added thoughtfully, "I might spend a few days at Stoverton, see how the work I ordered is being carried out."

"Just make sure you're back by Friday," Lady Barbara said. "The Devereaux ball is that night and the Prince is expected to attend."

"All right." Evan stood and left the library on his way to the small dining room where breakfast was served. He hoped very much Julia was not there. He needed time to adjust to the thought that she wasn't his cousin after all.

Chapter Twenty-Eight

Evan managed to get away from Althorpe house before he saw Julia. He drove the curricle with Sammy perched up behind him, and, as the day was warm and sunny and the roads were good, the trip was accomplished by early afternoon.

Driving under the blue Kent skies, Evan had gone over and over in his mind just how to broach this subject with the earl. Then he had worried the earl wouldn't be at home. He also wondered what kind of man could father a child on another man's wife, then leave the girl's future to the mercy of an unknown American.

Evan wasn't as overpowered by the neo-classical magnificence of the huge stone mansion that was Sheffield Manor as he would have been a few months ago. He drove the curricle to the front door of the main three-story block and went up the stairs to stand between two massive columns and raise the knocker. When the footman opened the door, he introduced himself with ease and was invited into a neo-classical hall, its pale green color setting off a delicate plasterwork ceiling. The footman showed him into a small drawing room off the hall and told him he would see if the earl was available.

When Edward Winston, Earl of Sheffield, walked into the room ten minutes later, Evan rose from his seat on one of those small gilt chairs he so disliked. "How do you do, my lord," he said. "I am sorry to interrupt your day, but I come on a matter of some importance. It concerns your son."

The Earl of Sheffield was an older man than Evan had expected. He was slender, of medium height, and his full head of hair was gray. He carried a cane. He approached Evan without using it and grasped his hand in a firm handshake. Evan looked into eyes that were gray like Julia's only darker. Before he could stop himself, he exclaimed, "My God, you look just like her."

The earl's expression didn't change. "She looks like me would be the proper way to phrase it."

Evan took a deep breath. The sight of the earl had left no doubt he might have about Julia's parentage.

The earl said, "Come along to the library, Althorpe. We can be private there."

Evan followed the older man down a long corridor, past a dining room that could have seated 50 people, to a book-lined room that looked out on the back garden.

"Sit please," the earl said, going toward a cabinet in the corner that reminded Evan of the cabinet in Althorpe House. "Wine or brandy?"

"Brandy, please."

The earl brought him a glass then seated himself in a comfortable leather chair opposite Evan. "This is about Tom, you said?"

"Yes. Sir Gordon and Lady Barbara have sent me to ask you to call him home from London. Apparently he and Lady Julia like each other rather too much for my aunt and uncle's comfort. You will, of course, understand their concern."

The earl had taken brandy as well and he drank off half the glass. "I didn't know Julia was in London."

"She is having a season with my cousin, Elizabeth Lewis."

"A season? Don't tell me Gordon Lewis is paying for Julia to have a season?"

"He isn't. I am. Julia needs to find a husband, but clearly your son is not an appropriate choice."

"Damn. This is the last thing I wanted to happen." The earl's mouth set in a grim line. "Of course I'll get him home. Has their being together caused much gossip?"

"I don't know. But my aunt is concerned. Julia doesn't like very many people, you see, and she quite clearly likes your son. They're both mad about horses and hunting."

"They get that from me," the earl said. He lifted his cane and smiled ruefully. "Didn't quite make it over a fence one day."

190

Evan stared at the slender aristocrat sitting across from him and anger swelled inside his chest. "Do you know the kind of life she's had? Do you know she and Maria were left virtually alone in that house for months on end? Do you know that Julia found her fa...my uncle's body? He had blown his face away, by the way. A nice thing for a young girl to come across on a morning stroll through the garden!"

The earl had gone white at this last statement. "I knew that Helen wanted her at Stoverton. Julia looked too much like me, she said. She also said that Julia loved being at Stoverton, that it was no hardship for the child to remain in the country."

"It's not the fact that she lived in the country that's the issue. When I arrived at Stoverton she and Maria and an elderly cousin were living in four unheated rooms—Julia had not enough money to pay for coal. They were wearing old clothes that didn't fit and were dependent upon the good graces of the local gentry to send them meat."

The earl looked stricken. "That only happened after Helen died. When she was alive she saw to it that Julia and her sister were taken care of. When they were left to Althorpe's care alone, there was nothing I could do. If I had tried to intervene, the gossip would have been brutal, and Julia would never find a husband. When Althorpe himself died I did the only thing I could, I sent Julia an allowance through her attorney and had him tell her it was coming from one of her father's accounts. I wanted to send a great deal more, but it would have looked suspicious to her."

"So that's where the money came from," Evan exclaimed. "Althorpe was totally ruined, so I knew it couldn't be coming from the estate. And Mr. Shields was admirably silent on the subject."

"Good man," the earl said.

Evan's mouth set in a grim line. "From what my aunt tells me, everyone in town already knew about your affair with Julia's mother. So why would your helping her ruin her chances?"

"There's a difference between *knowing* and knowing. As long as the fiction of her paternity is maintained, Julia will be accepted. Believe me, Althorpe, there are many aristocratic children who call the wrong man 'father,' and we all look the other way. But if the rules are flouted, if the children are acknowledged to be bastards, then society will turn its back. So it's best to play by the rules."

Evan felt sick to his stomach at this hypocrisy. "In America we take marriage seriously. My father married my mother in the teeth of his family's opposition, and my parents loved each other until the day they died!"

The earl did not look impressed. "That is certainly admirable," he said dryly, "but your father was a younger son. He didn't have the weight of a dynasty on his back. When duty dictates you must marry someone you don't love – perhaps someone you don't even like – you do what you must for the sake of the family. And if you find love elsewhere, you take what you can get."

Evan stared at the man sitting opposite him as if he was an alien creature. "And I'll bet you all go faithfully to church on Sunday to give a 'good example' to your tenants. It's hypocrisy, pure and simple."

"It's the reality of an old world," the earl said. "You're a new country; you have opportunities and choices we who live in the old world do not. But you have been called upon to take up the burdens of our world. You are the Earl of Althorpe, owner of a huge estate with many hundreds of people depending upon you for their livelihoods. When you make your choices you must keep in mind your responsibilities. You are taking your responsibility for Julia and Maria seriously, and I applaud that. But what of Stoverton? What are your plans for what should be one of the greatest estates in the country?"

Evan did not care for this interrogation and spoke stiffly, "I am investing a great deal of money in Stoverton. The tenant farms and cottages are a disgrace."

The earl smiled slightly. "They are, and I am pleased to hear you are investing in repairs. So you are planning to make England your home."

It was not a question, but Evan answered as if it was. "No. I am not staying in England. I plan to return to America, which *is* my home."

The earl's smile disappeared. Evan found it a little disconcerting to have Julia's eyes look at him with such disappointment and disapproval.

Sheffield said, "Stoverton cannot survive if it is once again burdened with an absentee landlord. Your uncle was a disgrace to his name. If you had known him you would understand why Helen looked elsewhere for affection. He neglected his wife and he neglected his duty to his own people. Do you think your father, who grew up at Stoverton and loved it, would want you to walk away from his family's heritage?"

"My father was a loyal American!"

"Good for him, I say. He was the best of the family, but there was nothing here for him except the army or the church. That's the fate of younger sons here in England. Your father escaped it, he married the woman he loved and he made himself a new life and a fortune. Good for him, I say. But, what do you think he would do if he were in your position, Evan? Would he walk away from his responsibilities knowing that so many people depended upon him?"

Evan could not tell this man that he had planned to put Julia in charge of the work at Stoverton. Sheffield would be horrified. Evan believed that Julia was capable, but he was also beginning to think that in his own way he was failing her as badly as her parents had. He was asking her to marry someone she didn't love so she could take on the burden that rightly belonged to him. He was asking her to do the very thing he said he most abhorred.

He hadn't wanted to become the Earl of Althorpe. He hadn't wanted to shoulder an enormous responsibility like Stoverton.

But…would his father say it was his duty to take up this burden? Evan had the uncomfortable feeling that he would.

It was a somber and irresolute Evan who drove away from Sheffield that afternoon. The unthinkable had become the possible. How could he bear to remain in England for the rest of his life?

On the other hand, how could he bear never to see Julia again? It was time to confront his feelings for her and stop fooling himself.

Her face was so distinct in his mind. Her features, so sharply cut yet so delicate. The wry twist of her lips when she teased him. Her smile. The long stem of her beautiful neck. Her eyes.

His body stirred and his breath caught.

Julia, he thought. Julia – who was not his cousin.

Chapter Twenty-Nine

Evan left Sheffield and with a perturbed mind he directed Sammy to drive to Stoverton. Toby was lunging Isabella when they drove in and he looked at Evan with alarm.

"Your lordship! We wasn't expecting you."

"I know," Evan said. "I was in the neighborhood and thought I'd stop by." He jumped down from the curricle's seat. "Take care of the horses," he said to Sammy. "I'll walk to the house. It'll feel good to stretch my legs."

"Yes, my lord," Sammy said, and gave Toby an inquiring look. Toby said, "I'll finish exercising Isabella and you take care of the horses, Sammy."

Evan began to walk down the graveled pathway that led from the stables to the house. In the late afternoon light, Stoverton appeared almost a fantasy, a golden palace haloed by a blue and gold sky streaked with long white clouds. The grass needed to be cut which made the house look as if it was floating on a sea of green.

Evan stopped and looked at his family home for a long time. The size was no longer as overwhelming to him as it had been when he first beheld it. And it was beautiful. He acknowledged that to himself, if somewhat reluctantly. The vision before him was a bit like that painting by Turner he had liked so much.

The front door was locked, and Evan rapped the knocker several times. No one answered. He went around the house to the kitchen door and knocked there. Mrs. Pierce opened the door slightly, saw who it was and went white. Evan, afraid she was going to faint, pushed the door opened and grabbed her arms to hold her up.

"Are you all right?"

"My lord…. Is it really you?"

"Yes. I'm sorry to have startled you but my decision to come was rather sudden."

Color began to come back into the cook's face, and Evan let go of her arms. Steps sounded on the uncarpeted wood stairs and then Lucy was in the kitchen staring at Evan with huge round eyes.

"My lord!"

"Where is Peter?" Evan asked. The footman had been left behind and Evan had expected him to open the door.

"His pa died, my lord, and he went home for the funeral. We didn't think to see you…"

"I see. Of course he should have gone home, but I am so sorry to have frightened you." He gave them his most charming smile. "Is it possible for me to have a cup of tea, Mrs. Pierce?"

"Accourse, my lord! Accourse! I'll put the kettle right on. Where do you want it served?""

Evan sat at the kitchen table, favored them with another heart-rending smile, and said, "Here, if you don't mind."

Mrs. Pierce beamed. "Accorse not, my lord. And I have some fresh pie as well."

"That sounds wonderful," Evan said sincerely.

The cook sent Lucy to make up the bed in the earl's room and get a fire going in the library. Evan drank his tea, ate his pie, and went upstairs to the deserted house.

He walked around the empty rooms. The furniture was swathed in white Holland covers making the house look and feel like a haven for ghosts. Yet people had lived here for centuries. These rooms had once been full of gaiety and conversation and laughter. He remembered Cousin Flora's stories of the wonderful Christmases she had spent here as a child.

On impulse, Evan went into the old part of the house and up the stairs to the long gallery. The pictures had not been re-covered when they left for London and he walked down the gallery, looking carefully at each of the portraits hung on the chestnut paneled walls. The family resemblance from one portrait to the next was remarkable. There was a picture of a young girl dressed in seventeenth-century garb who looked amazingly like Frances had looked at that age. The gallery also presented an array of family pets. Evidently the Marshalls had always been dog lovers. He had had a dog when he was a boy, but he had been away at sea for so much of his adult life that a pet hadn't been feasible.

He stopped for a long time to look at the picture of his father as a boy surrounded by his family. The eldest son, Philip, looked to be about twelve and his face was solemn as he stood next to his mother's chair. There was no sign on that boyish face of the character flaw that would lead him to gamble away his inheritance. Evan's father, who must have been nine or ten, looked as if he was ready to burst into motion as soon as he was released from his pose. Evan smiled. He remembered that leashed energy of his father's very well. Aunt Barbara was just a pretty blonde-haired blue-eyed little girl.

Evan moved on to the next picture, a portrait of Julia's parents with their children. The late countess was a petite woman whose hand on Julia's shoulder looked a trifle stiff, as if it wasn't an accustomed gesture. Her hair was black and there was something formidable in her steady hazel gaze.

He looked at Julia's mother for a long time, then he looked at the son who had drowned so tragically. His eyes were blue and he had the Marshall nose and chin. There was another boy older than Julia, but Maria was not in the picture. Presumably she hadn't been born when it was painted.

His father had grown up in this house. As had his mother. It was a strange feeling to think about that. It was a strange feeling to think of generation after generation of his family living here over the centuries.

Evan had the eerie feeling that the eyes of all the Marshalls in the room were looking at him. Challenging him. It made him uncomfortable to turn his back and walk away.

He remained at Stoverton for a week, spending most of his time on the farms, walking the land because Baron was in London and he wasn't going to attempt to ride Isabella. He found that being on foot made it easier for him to see the neglect up close. It also made it easier for him to get to know his tenants, and he spent hours in shabby farm kitchens listening to what they had to say.

By the time Evan was ready to leave Stoverton he had realized the truth of Lord Sheffield's warning. Stoverton could not survive with an absentee landlord. Someone needed to be here: to supervise the repairs to the house; to see about repairs to the tenants' cottages; to see about the needs of the farmland, which was the source of Stoverton's income.

He had planned for Julia and her phantom husband to be the ones in charge. It had been an insane idea, he thought, as he sat in front of the library fire on his last night in his father's old home. Not that he doubted Julia's capability; after all, he had a sister who ran a huge shipping business. What had been insane was his idea that she should marry someone to make her look respectable. He thought of the men who called at the house to see her, who danced with her at the balls. The only one with whom she was remotely compatible had turned out to be her brother!

Evan had never been a possessive man, but he was finding that his feelings for Julia were possessive in the extreme. He would never hand her over to one of those simpering dandies who hung around her in London. Julia was going to marry him.

And so, as he sat by the fire that evening, Evan Marshall came to the conclusion that he, the Earl of Althorpe, the man who was responsible for the lives of so many people, the man who loved Julia, would have to remain in England and do his duty.

*

When Evan returned to London he went straight to the office of Mr. Rothschild. The young solicitor was delighted to see him.

"I've found a way to break the entail," he said as soon as Evan was seated in the heavy wood chair on the far side of the solicitor's large, paper-strewn desk.

Evan stared into the intelligent dark eyes of his attorney. If he could get money out of the London house...he inhaled deeply. "Are you certain?"

"Yes." The young man stood and went unerringly to one of the piles of papers stacked on a table against the wall. He brought them to the desk, selected one page in particular, and handed it Evan. "If you will read this section, my lord, you will see how the entail can be set aside."

Evan read it carefully and didn't see. Mr. Rothschild explained in detail, and then Evan understood. He leaned forward to ask the most important question: "Will the courts agree with you?"

"Oh, yes, my lord. I've already checked with a few of my colleagues. The whole process will be made simpler because there is no other heir in sight to challenge your request. You can break the entail on both the house and the furnishings."

Evan's mouth dropped open. "The house too?"

"The house too."

"How long will this take? What do you think the house would fetch? What about the paintings? What are they worth?"

Mr. Rothschild laughed and held up his hand. "One question at a time, my lord."

Evan grinned at him. "Sorry, but this is such a wonderful surprise. It might mean I won't have to mortgage Stoverton."

"Let me explain how this will proceed," Mr. Rochschild said, and Evan settled down to listen.

Chapter Thirty

When I learned that Evan had gone down to Stoverton. I was furious. When I expressed my feelings to Lizzie, she was sympathetic.

"I know it seems rotten to you, Julia, but it wouldn't be proper for you to travel alone with Evan without a chaperone."

"He's my cousin!" I said indignantly.

"A cousin isn't a brother, particularly a cousin who is a young, eligible, single male."

"That's ridiculous."

"It's not."

"Evan's an American. He's different."

Lizzie sighed. "I know how much you miss Stoverton, but Evan simply could not take you with him, Julia. He's a supremely eligible bachelor and in England first cousins can marry."

I didn't know that. I hadn't really thought about it.

It doesn't matter, I told myself firmly. Even if he should be interested in me, he's going back to America. I have to be here to take care of Stoverton.

This whole conversation with Lizzie depressed me unutterably. London seemed duller than ever, and when I attended two more balls, and Tom was at neither of them, my depression only deepened.

"Do you know what happened to Tom Winston, Aunt Barbara?" I asked as we sat at breakfast the morning after the stupendously boring ball I had suffered through the evening before.

"I believe he went home," my aunt said off-handedly. "He's not fond of London, as you know."

I knew he wasn't fond of London, but I had thought he was fond of me. It hurt that he hadn't bothered to call to say goodbye. I liked him. He never made me feel as Evan did when I danced with him, but I liked him. He was good company.

"Oh," I said gloomily.

Aunt Barbara said, "I do believe Ormesby is interested in you, Julia. He always asks you to dance."

I knew Ormesby wasn't interested in me. He found me amusing, but he wasn't interested in marrying me. I decided it would be unwise to say as much to Aunt Barbara, so I just put a large forkful of eggs into my mouth and chewed. Lizzie, bless her, took over the conversation.

*

That afternoon, after luncheon, Lizzie found me in the stable feeding carrots to Ty. "May I speak to you for a moment, Julia?" she asked.

"Of course." I gave Ty the final carrot and he nickered after me as I walked away with Lizzie.

"Come up to my room," she said.

When we were both sitting in the comfortable chairs in front of the mantelpiece she said, "I need your help, Julia."

"Of course," I said, mystified by her pleading expression. "What do you want me to do?

"Help me to meet Roger without Mama knowing."

My mouth fell opened and my eyes popped. "Roger? As in *Lord* Roger, the duke's brother?"

"Yes. You haven't noticed anything between us?"

"No," I replied, my eyes still popping.

"Good. I'm glad we haven't seemed obvious."

I said truthfully, "Lizzie, I have been so miserable lately that I wouldn't have noticed if the two of you started kissing on the ballroom floor. Are you in love with Lord Roger?"

Lizzie lifted her chin. "Yes, I am. And I know he loves me. I just have to arrange a way for him to tell me so."

I was hardly the person to consult about affairs of the heart, but I didn't want to stop her from confiding in me. "What about the duke?" I asked.

"I have to get rid of the duke," she replied.

I envisioned shooting him as he rode in the park. I knew the exact place where I could hide...

Lizzie was going on, "Roger hasn't realized that his brother is paying attention to me, and I haven't mentioned it. If he did know, I'm afraid he'd step back. He adores his big brother, you see. It's very annoying."

Roger seemed a poor-spirited sort of suitor to me, but I had enough sense not to say that to Lizzie.

She went on, "Roger is so very smart in some ways, but in other ways...well, he doesn't always *notice* things. He's seen the duke dance with me, of course, but he hasn't yet tumbled to the fact that his brother might be serious."

"Do you think he *is* serious?"

Lizzie looked at me mournfully. "Yes, I do."

"But you don't want to marry him."

"No, I want to marry Roger."

I smiled. "Lizzie, your mama will have a seizure if you reject a duke and marry a clergyman."

"Julia," she looked very stern, "we cannot allow the duke to propose. That would be fatal to all my hopes."

Roger was sounding less and less of a prize. "Are you certain you love him?" I asked.

"I love him terribly. He's a truly splendid young man, Julia. He's brilliant, but he also cares deeply about people. He'll make a wonderful shepherd for his flock." She gave me an earnest blue stare. "And I think I would make a good clergyman's wife. It's a much more useful and satisfying position than being a duchess."

I looked at my beautiful cousin and realized she was right. No one was kinder or more generous or more compassionate than Lizzie. "You would be a perfect clergyman's wife," I said.

She smiled radiantly.

"He hasn't asked you to marry him?"

"No. He's so diffident, Julia. I'm going to have to ask him – if we can only be alone long enough for me to do it!"

She was going to ask him. Good for Lizzie.

"What do you want me to do?"

"I mentioned to him last night that I would be walking in the park at three this afternoon. I think he'll be there too. Will you come with me?"

"Of course I will."

Lizzie's eyes grew misty. "He's so handsome—his eyes and mouth are so grave and serious and yet, when he smiles..." She sighed.

"He's a beautiful man," I said, banishing from my mind the picture of the one truly beautiful man I knew.

Lizzie hugged me and we made our plans.

Chapter Thirty-One

True to my word, I walked with Lizzie to the park that afternoon, and, at the last minute, Maria and Miss Dixon came with us. It was an unusually cold day and there were few people on the path. We had all dressed sensibly, however, and we walked bravely into the wind, inhaling the clean air of the park, which was far more pleasant than the air in most of London.

Lord Roger appeared halfway through our walk, coming from the opposite direction. Lizzie asked him to join us and, after offering a delightfully shy smile to the rest of us, he did. Lizzie gave me a look and I slowed down, holding Maria's arm so she would slow down with me. Lizzie and Lord Roger walked faster, and we followed at a distance.

Maria half-whispered, "What's happening between Lizzie and Lord Roger?"

"Nothing as of yet," I murmured. "She wants to make something happen, though, and we need to give her some privacy."

Maria's blue eyes were huge. "Does Lizzie *love* him?"

I nodded.

Miss Dixon looked shocked. "But the duke…."

"The devil with the duke," I said. "Lizzie is much too good a person to be a duchess."

Miss Dixon laughed, and her eyes danced. "Only think what Lady Barbara will say."

I smiled with satisfaction.

We walked on in silence for a while, our eyes fixed on the couple in front of us. They slowed, then stopped and turned toward us. "I'm going to show Lord Roger that patch of wild blueberries we came across the other day. Would you mind waiting for us, Julia?"

"Of course not. I'm a little fatigued anyway."

As Lizzie led Lord Roger down a narrow trail that led into deep woods, Maria said, "What a whisker, Julia. You're never fatigued!"

"A blueberry patch in Hyde Park," Miss Dixon said. She was smiling. "How fascinating."

I pointed to a near-by bench. "Let's sit and give Lizzie some time to bring Lord Roger up to scratch."

We sat for half an hour trying to ignore the cold. Maria was shivering and I was beginning to think Lizzie was never going to return from the mythical blueberry bush when she and Roger finally stepped out onto the path. Lizzie was glowing. You could warm your hands at her smile, I thought.

I grinned at her. "Do you have news to share?"

"Yes. But we're going to keep it a secret until I can get Papa back to London. Roger needs to speak to him."

"What about the duke? Maria blurted.

Roger smiled at her. He really was a handsome young man and right now he looked almost as radiant as Lizzie. "I'll tell him, of course. He won't believe his little brother snagged the prettiest girl in England, but he'll be happy for me. He's always been my greatest supporter in the family."

Miss Dixon and I exchanged glances.

"Of course he'll be happy," Lizzie said. "How could he be otherwise?"

This was true. The duke could hardly admit that he had been beaten out by his scholarly little brother. After all, I thought, it was his own fault for taking too long to make Lizzie an offer.

*

I was happy for Lizzie, but my own life had turned into a sad muddle. Evan had laid out a huge amount of money to find me a husband and so far the only person who was even remotely acceptable had disappeared from London without a word. I wanted desperately to go back to Stoverton, but somehow the thought of living there by myself wasn't as appealing as it once had been.

I told myself I would have felt differently if I was marrying Tom Winston. Sir Matthew would love Tom. He would fit very well into Stoverton, and I was certain he would be a help to me in getting the farms back into full production. *And* he had promised he would wangle me a ride with the Quorn. Tom had said that once Mr. Assheton Smith, the Master, saw how well I rode, I would be welcome to join them whenever I wished.

But the truth was, I didn't miss Tom the way I missed Evan. Tom didn't light up a room just by walking into it. I couldn't meet Tom's eyes and know exactly what he was thinking, the way I could with Evan. Tom didn't make my heart beat faster when he touched me.

I was in a dismal mood when the morning post came the next day. I had just come down the stairs and I said to the footman who was holding the postal delivery, "I'm going to the dining room, Sidney. I'll take it to her ladyship."

"Thank you, Lady Julia," he replied and gave me the bundle.

As I walked down the hall I riffled casually through the various notes; then I stopped as suddenly as if I had run into glass. Aside from the usual invitations there were two letters. One was addressed to my aunt and was sent from Stoverton.

Hope flared in my heart. Perhaps Evan was writing to say he was coming back to London. I walked faster, wanting to hear what he had written, but before I went into the dining room I glanced at the second letter in my hand. It was addressed to me. I halted and looked at the name of the sender. It had come from Sheffield.

Tom, I thought. Fortunately I was wearing a dress with pockets and I quickly slipped the letter out of sight. I had a prescient feeling that Aunt Barbara would not allow me to receive a letter from a gentleman unless she had first read it herself.

I put Evan's letter and the invitations in front of Aunt Barbara and took my place at table. There was a rack of buttered toast in front of me and I put one slice on my plate and accepted a cup of tea from the footman.

Aunt Barbara opened the letter, perused it, and looked up at Lizzie and me. "Evan will be returning to London later today." She sounded pleased. "It's certainly time. We have sorely missed the company of a gentleman."

My heart leaped in my chest. He was coming back today! Suddenly, I was hungry. There were eggs, sausages and muffins on the sideboard, and I piled them on my plate and began to eat with an appetite I had not known in days.

It wasn't until breakfast was finished and I was going back upstairs that I thought of Tom's letter. What if Tom had gone home to speak to his father about me? What if he was going to propose? What if I had to marry him?

Once that happened, Evan would go back to America and I would never see him again. I trailed upstairs to my room feeling the cloud of heavy misery that had been my companion ever since Evan left settle over me again. My future looked bleak indeed.

Chapter Thirty-Two

I walked slowly into my bedroom and took Tom's letter out of my pocket. A small sofa nestled under the window and I sat to get the outdoor light.

I remained for a while, just staring at the letter and talking to myself. Being married to Tom won't be that bad. He's nice and he's fun to be with and I'll be living at Stoverton, which is all I've ever wanted. He'll fit in there perfectly. We can go hunting together and ride across the estate together…

This was where my positive thinking stumbled. If we're married, I'll have to sleep with him.

I liked Tom, but I didn't want to sleep with him.

I'd like to sleep with Evan.

I looked quickly around, afraid that someone might have heard my thought. My heart was beating like a drum, but no one was in the room except me. I was the person afraid of my thought, afraid of what it revealed.

I covered my face with my hands. This was terrible. How had I gone from hating the unknown American who was stealing my heritage to loving him? I had never been good at dissembling; how was I to face Evan with this knowledge in my heart?

I sat in the sun as it streamed through the window and thought back over the months we had known each other. I thought of the things we had done, the times we had been together, and I came to the conclusion that Evan wasn't indifferent to me either. There was something between us, and he sensed it as well as I.

But what was to be done? Evan was going back to America and I was certain he wouldn't want to take me with him. What good would I be to him in America? What good would I be to myself? I wasn't a very adaptable person and I would probably make the both of us miserable.

And I had a duty to Stoverton. I was the only Marshall left who cared about it. I couldn't let it fall into decay while I sailed off to

Massachusetts. If I ever was asked to sail to Massachusetts, which was unlikely.

The letter I still held in my hand was sticking into my cheek and I lifted my face and smoothed it out. Then I opened it and began to read.

> *Dear Julia,*
>
> *I have thought long and hard about whether I should write you this letter, but I have decided you are entitled to know why I left London so abruptly. My father has ordered me not to communicate with you, but one of the grooms is posting this letter from the local inn.*
>
> *I have never liked a girl as much as I like you, and I know you like me in return. It was this mutual affection that caused my hasty removal from London. There are some facts that you and I were not aware of, and I think you should be made cognizant of them.*
>
> *My father, the Earl of Sheffield, is your father as well. He and your mother had a long-term affair and you were the result of that relationship. As your mother was married, her husband had little choice but to accept you as his own child. Unfortunately, this sort of thing is not uncommon among the English upper class.*
>
> *I have told you this because I didn't want you to think that I had simply lost interest and discarded you. I would never do such a thing. What happened was that your aunt became alarmed at the closeness she saw between us and wrote to my father, telling him that he should call me home.*
>
> *I hope I have done the right thing in confiding this information to you. My reason was purely selfish—I like my new sister far too much to lose her. With our relationship on a new footing, perhaps we can actually hunt with the Quorn together one day.*
>
> *Your loving brother,*
>
> *Tom*

I read the letter once. Then I read it again, and then one more time. It wasn't until I had looked at that signature for the third time that I fully comprehended what Tom—my brother—had told me.

I wasn't a Marshall. There was not a drop of Marshall blood in my body. For all the years of my life I had been living a lie. I was the bastard child of another man, and it was only my father's—my *fake* father's—willingness to allow me into his family that had saved me from being labeled a bastard.

I was stunned. Frozen. Aunt Barbara knew about this. Who else knew? I saw the faces of the patronesses of Almack's pass before my eyes. They knew. They must know. Those women of the world knew everything. And my mother had been a patroness herself; she had been their friend.

I'm not a Marshall.

I had built my whole life on being a Marshall, on carrying the blood of a great English family in my veins. Being a Marshall was what I was—who I was. I had been deceived. I had no right to Stoverton. I had no right to anything or anyone. I was no one. I was a lie.

I looked around the large, pretty room, with its comfortable bed, elegantly carved mantelpiece and thick expensive rug. I couldn't stay here. I didn't belong here. How could I look my supposed aunt in the face? How could I go on pretending that Lizzie was my cousin and Maria my sister? How could I ever face Evan?

I couldn't stay here, but where could I go? I had nobody. I wasn't Lady Julia Marshall; I was an imposter. No one would take me in.

Every fiber of my being wanted to flee to Stoverton—my safe place, my beloved home. But I had no right to Stoverton. I wasn't a Marshall. I was a bastard...a Nothing.

And then I thought of Sir Matthew. He had been the only father I had ever known. He would take me in. He would help me decide what I should do. I'd sneak out to the stable, saddle up Ty, and ride to Sir Matthew's house.

Then I thought of Maria. How could I run away and leave Maria? She would be so frightened for me. She would feel as if I had deserted her.

Lizzie will take care of Maria. I can depend on Lizzie to do the right thing.

My eyes filled with tears as I pictured my little sister—a perfect Marshall with her blue eyes and golden hair. For so many years it had been just the two of us. But I couldn't take care of her anymore. I didn't even know if I could take care of myself. I would leave her a note telling her not to worry, that I had found out some upsetting news and was going away for a while. I would write to her when I had sorted things out.

I wrote the letter and propped it on the mantel in my bedroom. Then I went to the wardrobe, took down a small brown bag that would attach to my saddle, and began to pack the few things I would need.

Chapter Thirty-Three

When Evan returned to the London house later that afternoon, he found his family in an uproar.

Lizzie met him at the door and grabbed his hand. "Evan, thank God you have come! The most dreadful thing has happened. Julia's disappeared!"

Evan stared down into her face as if he hadn't understood. "What do you mean, 'disappeared?' She's probably down in the stable with Ty."

Lizzie shook her head frantically. "No, she isn't. But Ty is gone too."

The sound of light footsteps on the marble floor announced the arrival of Maria. "Is Julia at Stoverton?" she demanded. When he shook his head, she threw herself into his arms and began to cry.

Evan looked over her golden head to Lizzie. Lizzie said, "She left Maria a note. She wrote she had learned something upsetting and was going to go away for a while."

She found out. It was Evan's immediately thought. But how the hell had she found out? Sheffield wasn't the kind of man to tell her....

He put Maria away from him gently and asked Lizzie, "Has Tom Winston been in town lately?"

Lizzie frowned in bewilderment. "No, he hasn't. In fact, Julia was irked that he left without speaking to her. Do you think that's why she ran away? Because I don't agree, Evan. She didn't love Tom Winston. They were only friends. She wasn't at all upset by Tom's leaving; she was just a little...well, irked."

"Has Julia received any letters recently?" he asked, looking from Lizzie to Maria.

Both girls shook their heads.

"I must speak to your Mama," he said to Lizzie. "Where is she?"

"She's in the morning room. She's very worried about this, Evan."

"She damn well should be," he replied grimly and strode down the hallway, still garbed in his caped driving cloak.

Lady Barbara was seated at the elegant French desk that was placed between two windows, but she swung around when she heard the door open. She rose to her feet and went toward her nephew echoing her daughter's words of a few moments ago, "Evan! Thank God you have come."

"How long has she been missing?" he demanded, without even greeting her.

"Since yesterday morning. That wretched boy must have communicated with her somehow. It's all I can think of to account for her acting in such an outrageous way. Where can she have gone?"

"She didn't go to Stoverton. I only left there a few hours ago and I didn't see her."

Lady Barbara turned white. "Oh no. I was so hoping that was where she went."

The door opened and Lizzie and Maria came in. Lady Barbara turned to them and said in her most chilling and autocratic voice, "I do not want you girls in this room. Go to the library and wait for us there."

Lizzie came in and sat on the gold tapestry sofa. "I am not going anywhere, Mama. I love Julia and I want to do everything I can to help find her."

"Your cousin and I will figure this out between us," Lady Barbara said. "Go to the library, Elizabeth."

Maria joined Lizzie on the sofa. "Julia is my sister. She's all I have in the world." A heartbreaking little sob caught in her throat and she looked at Evan with huge blue eyes. "You have to find her, Evan. You *have* to."

"What could have upset her so much that she would do this?" Lizzie asked. "It's not like Julia. She would never leave Maria."

Evan rubbed his eyes and leaned his shoulders against the pale green wall beside the mantelpiece. He looked from his aunt to the two girls on the sofa. "It's an ugly story and Julia should never have heard it."

"What story?" Lizzie demanded. "Does it have to do with Tom Winston?"

"I'm afraid it does," Evan said.

"*Althorpe!* Lady Barbara's voice was outraged. "Do not dare repeat this story to my daughter. Do you hear me? This is not for the ears of young girls."

"If Julia had to hear it, then I want to hear it too," Maria said. "She's my *sister!* The only person who ever loved me. I want to know!"

"Absolutely not," Lady Barbara said. "Both of you go to your rooms."

Neither girl moved. Evan said, "You English have the most peculiar ideas about young women. Neither Lizzie nor Maria will be corrupted by what I have to say, Aunt Barbara. They're intelligent young women and they're deeply worried about Julia. So am I, and they might have some idea about where she went if they know what has happened."

"Evan, I forbid you..." Lady Barbara began.

Evan's voice over-rode hers. "Aunt Barbara and Uncle Gordon were concerned about the relationship that appeared to be growing between Julia and Tom Winston. They sent me down to Sheffield Manor to inform Tom's father of the situation and to ask him to call Tom home from London. Lord Sheffield did so."

"But why did Tom have to go home?" Lizzie asked.

"Because Tom's father, Lord Sheffield, is Julia's father as well." Evan looked at Maria and his voice gentled. "Your mother had an affair with Lord Sheffield and that is how Julia was conceived. She and Tom are half brother and sister."

Lady Barbara moaned, threw herself into a chair and covered her eyes.

"Good heavens," Lizzie said, wide-eyed.

"It's just like *Oedipus Rex*," Maria said.

"What's that?" Lizzie asked.

Maria turned to her cousin and explained, "*Oedipus Rex*, is a play about a man who marries his mother without knowing she's his mother."

"I never got to read that!" Lizzie said.

"Oh My God!" Lady Barbara cried. "What is happening to my child?"

Evan continued. "Lord Sheffield promised me he would instruct Tom not to communicate with Julia, but I'm certain he must have. There's nothing else I can imagine that would have thrown her into such a state."

Maria said slowly, "She found out she wasn't a Marshall."

"Yes," Evan said.

"Oh Evan." Maria had tears in her eyes. "Julia has always been so proud of being a Marshall. She knows everything about the family. She can tell you the name of every earl and what he did and what his children did too. This news must have been devastating."

Maria had not said anything Evan didn't already know. He said, "Julia's whole world has been turned upside down and she had to get away from us. Maria, think. Where might she go? She wouldn't go to Stoverton because she'd feel she didn't belong there anymore. Is there anywhere else she might have sought refuge?"

Maria bent her head, thinking hard. "If she couldn't go to Stoverton…" Her head jerked up. "She might have gone to the squire. Sir Matthew. She's very fond of him and he of her." Her face brightened. "I think that's where she must be, Evan. He'd take her in. His wife is dead, so he has no one else to consult. I think you should go to Sir Matthew's."

Evan looked at his aunt. "My horses are tired, Aunt Barbara. May I have two of your carriage horses harnessed to the curricle?"

Lady Barbara looked as if she had aged ten years. "Yes," she said. "You may."

*

Evan drank a cup of hot tea and ate some bread and cold roast beef while waiting for the horses to be harnessed. With Sammy sitting beside him, he drove southeast into Kent, along the same roads he had driven earlier in the opposite direction.

The sun was dropping in the sky by the time they reached their destination. The squire's house was a solid brick edifice with the front door placed symmetrically between three tall windows. Three perfectly spaced dormers peered down from the hipped roof. Evan scarcely glanced at it, however. He turned the curricle onto the graveled drive that wound around to the back of the house, where he expected to find the stables. He had a suspicion that if Julia was indeed here, she might have sought solace from the horses.

Just as Evan had thought, the stable, built of the same brick as the house, stood at the far end of a neatly scythed lawn. Evan had to discipline himself to keep the horses to a walk. Even from a distance he could see that there was someone in the stable yard with a horse. The horse was a bright chestnut and the girl was Julia.

She was bending over the horse's rear offside hoof, picking out the dirt. When she heard the sound of the curricle, she returned Ty's hoof to the ground and straightened up. Evan stopped the curricle only a few feet away and their eyes met.

He saw the blood drain from her face. He wanted to leap from the carriage, catch her in his arms and tell her not to be afraid, that he loved her and would take care of her forever. Her face told him this was not a good idea.

He swung down from the carriage and said as he walked toward her, "I thought I might find you here. You and I need to talk."

Chapter Thirty-Four

When I saw Evan walking toward me, it took every ounce of courage I had not to turn and run. Instead I stiffened my back, stood my ground, and answered him. "I don't want to talk to you. Go away."

"I have no intention of going anywhere," he replied, stopping directly in front of me.

As always, his height made me feel too small—I had to tilt my head way back to look up into his face. He was standing with his back to the west and the fading sun illuminated his hair. He was so beautiful, and I loved him so much, but I was not giving in to him. I still had some pride left.

"I want you to come back to Stoverton with me," he said.

I took a step away. I couldn't help myself. "I am never going to Stoverton again, and you know the reason why."

"Nonsense. You love Stoverton; it's your home."

"It's not my home," I said tightly. "I thought it was once, but I have no right to live there. I have no right to any say about what happens to it. I'm not a Marshall; I'm nothing."

He shook his head so forcefully a lock of hair fell forward onto his forehead, spangling it with silver. "Julia, you are very far from being nothing. You're one of the bravest, most gallant people I have ever known. And I was in a war, remember, so I know bravery and gallantry when I see it."

I couldn't keep looking at him so I turned my back and ran a hand along Ty's sleek neck. "How is Maria?" I asked, my voice muffled by the silky neck in front of me.

"How do you think she is? She's beside herself with fear for you. And for herself. Her exact words were that you were the only person who ever loved her, and I had to find you. In fact, it was she who had the idea that you might have sought refuge with Sir Matthew."

"Maria will be all right," I answered. "She's a Marshall. Lizzie will look after her."

"How do you know that Maria's a Marshall?"

A shock of surprise ran through me and I spun around to face him. "You only have to look at her to know her heritage!"

"The Marshalls are not the only blond, blue-eyed people in England, Julia. In fact, according to Aunt Barbara, Maria may well be the child of a Russian diplomat. A blond, blue-eyed Russian diplomat, who had great musical talent. Or so Aunt Barbara told me.

"I don't believe you," I said, but I did. If my mother had an affair with one man, why could she not have had an affair with another?

He shrugged. "What does it matter? Maria is Maria, a beautiful, talented sweetheart of a girl whom we all love. I don't care who her father was. In fact, I'm glad my uncle wasn't her father. Who would want to carry *his* blood in their veins?"

There was a pause as we stood there looking at each other. We both knew we weren't talking about Maria. I said, "Does all of London know about *Maria's* illegitimate birth?"

Again, he gave that casual shrug. "According to my aunt, the English aristocracy is packed with children whose father wasn't their mother's husband. Since this practice is so common, it's ignored. Apparently, as long as no one talks about it, it isn't there."

I heard a voice calling my name and looked across the lawn to see a broad, slightly bow-legged figure coming across the grass. "It's Sir Matthew," I said. "I don't believe you two have met."

Evan swung around to face the lawn and we both waited in silence until Sir Matthew reached us. He immediately put a protective hand on my shoulder and asked, "Are you all right, lass?"

I felt my eyes fill with tears. Tears. Me. I never used to cry and now it seemed as if I was crying all the time. But it was so sweet to know how much he cared for me.

I blinked the wretched tears back and said, "Sir Matthew, may I present the Earl of Athorpe, Evan Marshall."

I deliberately defied the rules of etiquette by introducing Evan to Sir Matthew instead of Sir Matthew to Evan. I knew Evan wouldn't care about the etiquette, but it made me feel good to give the honor to Sir Matthew.

Evan extended his hand and Sir Matthew took it.

"I have come to return Julia to her family, sir," Evan said.

He was the only peer in England who would have addressed Sir Matthew, a mere baronet, as 'sir.' I knew it was his American belief in equality, and I loved him for it.

Sir Matthew said, "Julia came to me because she discovered the truth about her birth, my lord. She is very distressed by what she has learned. May I ask what the family's intentions are toward Julia now?"

"They are as they have always been," Evan replied. "She was raised as the daughter of the Earl and Countess of Althorpe and so society and her family will continue to regard her. If I return her to London at once, no one need know about her abrupt departure."

Sir Matthew's hand pressed more firmly into my shoulder. "And what kind of future do *you* envision for her, my lord?"

I thought it was time to speak up for myself. "I don't want to marry any of those men I met in London. The only person I liked was Tom, and look what happened there!"

Evan gave me a long, blue look. "What *do* you want, Julia?"

I couldn't tell him what I wanted because what I wanted was impossible. "I want to remain here with Sir Matthew," I said defiantly.

Evan and Sir Matthew exchanged a long, silent look. Then Sir Matthew said quietly, "You haven't answered my question, my lord. What kind of future do you see for Julia?"

Evan's mouth set into a grim line. "This is not exactly how I planned to say this, but I suppose I must. I envision Julia's future to be with me. I want to marry her."

Sir Matthew dropped his hand from my shoulder and went to shake Evan's hand. "Good lad," he said, enthusiastically pumping away. "Good lad."

My head was spinning. Had Evan really said he wanted to marry me? I looked at the two men, shaking hands so heartily, as if they'd made a bargain between them.

Well, they had made a bargain, I thought. Evan felt sorry for me. He knew I had no place to go, so he had offered to take me on, the way he had offered to give me a season and bought me a horse. He felt responsible for me. And my darling Sir Matthew approved.

I would not allow it. My whole heart and body cried out for Evan, but I would not saddle him with a wife he didn't want, a wife who could only be a burden to him. A wife who was afraid to go to America.

I set my jaw and said, "Well, I don't want to marry you."

Once again the two men looked at each other over my head. I wanted to scream.

"I'll take her back to Stoverton with me for the night," Evan said to Sir Matthew. "No one needs to know we were there together. Then, tomorrow, I'll take her back to London."

I looked at Sir Matthew, knowing he would never agree to such an improper situation. "An excellent plan, my lord," he said. "I'll tell anyone who asks that Lady Julia was with me."

I couldn't believe what I was hearing. I looked at my dear and only friend and protested, "I can't be alone with Evan at Stoverton, Sir Matthew! It isn't proper."

Evan put his hand on my arm and started to march me toward the curricle. "I never thought to hear *you* worry about what was proper or improper, Julia."

I tried to pull away from him, but I couldn't.

Sir Matthew said, "I'll have someone bring Ty over to the Stoverton stables. Toby can look after him."

"Sammy can bring him," Evan said.

Sir Matthew nodded.

Evan picked me up as if I weighed nothing and plopped me in the curricle seat. He swung quickly into the driving seat, took up the reins and began to turn the horses. I looked over my shoulder at my protector. "Are you going to let him kidnap me, Sir Matthew?"

"Go along with you, lass, and listen to his lordship. He's a good'un and if you do as he says, you'll end up just fine."

The horses broke into a trot and I had to clutch the seat to keep my balance.

"I'm not going to talk to you," I said to the profile next to me.

"Well, I am going to talk to you," he replied, and the horses trotted faster.

Chapter Thirty-Five

I stared straight ahead during the drive and refused to speak. After making one or two attempts at conversation, Evan gave up. The entire drive was made in silence.

My first view of golden Stoverton almost broke my heart. I loved it so much that I wished I could stretch out my arms and embrace it.

Stop this, Julia, I told myself. You're an interloper here now. Stoverton belongs to Evan; there's no place for you at Stoverton any longer.

Evan stopped the horses in front of the great oak door and Peter came out almost immediately to help me down and take in the luggage. Evan was busy with the horses, so I took Peter's hand and jumped down from the seat.

"I don't have any luggage, Peter," I said coldly. "You can take his lordship's."

"I'm afraid I have no luggage either," Evan said. He had secured the horses' reins and descended from the high seat. "Lady Julia and I plan to stay just the one night. We'll be off to London in the morning."

Peter's eyebrows twitched, but he said only, "Very good, my lord. I shall have your bedroom and Lady Julia's prepared."

"Thank you," Evan said. He took my elbow into his large hand and prepared to march me into the house. I was not enamored of these strong man tactics and pulled my arm away. "I can walk by myself, thank you," I informed him, and swept ahead of him through the front door.

My heart cramped with love as I stood in the main hallway. Stoverton. I simply could not stop loving it even though I knew I had to put it behind me. It had belonged to a Marshall for many centuries and it must remain in the hands of a Marshall.

The hall was cold, but then we had stopped heating this part of the house during my mother's time.

My mother. I had tried not to think about her, about her betrayal of her husband and of Maria and me. She may not have loved my father—my *alleged* father—but she had sworn a solemn vow to be faithful to him.

I had no sympathy for my mother.

Evan took my elbow once again and guided me through the old part of the house. I didn't pull away this time—I needed his support. I would miss this house for the rest of my life.

We ended up in the library. Lucy was starting the fire as we came in the door and Evan said, "Will you make sure a fire is lit in my rooms, Lucy?"

She bobbed a curtsy, "Yes, my lord."

He hadn't told her to light a fire in my bedroom, but I held my tongue. I knew Lucy would take care of me.

The library door closed behind Peter leaving Evan and me alone. My heart began to beat faster, and I said, "There's no use in arguing, Evan. I will never marry you. I know you think you're obligated to offer for me, but my answer is no."

He didn't say anything, just stood looking at me with intent blue eyes, overpowering me with the force of his closeness. The air between us seemed to swell and throb and it took all my willpower to keep from moving toward him.

He said, "I don't want to marry you because I feel obligated to, I..."

I jumped in, cutting him off.

"I said I don't want to talk to you. I don't know why you insisted on bringing me here, but I am going to my room right now. I'll be ready for you to take me back to Sir Matthew's in the morning."

Evan's narrowed eyes had turned dark blue and were radiating such intensity that I shivered. He said, "Let's not talk then," and before I realized what was happening, he had pulled me into his arms and was kissing me. My whole body jolted at the touch of his mouth and, after a very brief moment, I kissed him back. I simply couldn't stop myself.

He kept kissing me and kissing me until I was so dizzy I couldn't think. My arms were around his waist and I clung to him, afraid I would fall apart if I let go.

Finally he lifted his head. He was breathing hard and the expression on his face stabbed into me like a knife. He said, "I don't want to marry you because I feel sorry for you. I want to marry you because I love you."

I had never heard such beautiful words. "You do?" My voice was shaky.

"Yes. I love you and I want to marry you. How about you, Julia?"

My heart was ringing like a cacophony of bells. He had said he loved me and I believed him. I rose on my toes and put my hands on his shoulders. "I love you too," I said and lifted my face to his.

This time his tongue pressed against my mouth and I opened my lips and let him in. The only light in the room was coming from the coals in the fire and the darkness seemed to breathe around us. The rhythm of his body beat against me and I pressed against him, filled with a fierce, aching passion I had not known existed.

When he put his hands on my shoulders and held me away, I almost stumbled. I looked up, not understanding his abrupt withdrawal. His face was hard with passion and his hair was disordered. Dimly I remembered running my hands through it. "Is something wrong?" I asked.

"We have to stop this Julia. If I keep kissing you like this I won't be able to stop at all."

He was such a wonderful man and I loved him so much. "Why should we stop?" I asked.

His eyes sparked blue fire and he stepped away from me, resisting temptation. "Because we're not married."

"But we're going to be married, aren't we?"

"We most certainly are, and as soon as possible."

"Then what difference does a few days, or weeks, make?" Part of me couldn't believe I was saying this, but a bigger part of me didn't care. We were here together, we could do as we pleased, and he was mine.

I could see him struggle to do the right thing – or what he thought to be the right thing. I took his hand and said, "Let's go to your bedroom."

Suddenly he grinned. "You are diabolical, do you know that?"

I smiled back. "That's why you love me."

He groaned. "God help me, it's true." He lifted my hand to his lips and kissed my palm. Then he folded my fingers over the kiss, picked me up and carried me to where I wanted to be.

*

The earl's bedroom had a fire just starting up in the fireplace. Evan laid me on the big bed and, as I looked up at him, the moonlight from the uncovered window fell upon him, silvering his hair and face. For a moment he looked like one of those Greek gods I had read about in the library here at Stoverton, but then he leaned over me, blocking the moonlight with his shoulders, and he was Evan again.

"You are so beautiful, Julia," he said, his voice thicker than usual. "Let me take that tie out of your hair."

I sat up a little so he could reach behind me to until the ribbon that held my hair away from my face. He smoothed one of the long shiny black locks between his fingers. "So beautiful," he said, and lifted the strand to his lips.

"You're the one who's beautiful," I said.

"I know – I look just like the first earl."

"No, you're much more beautiful than he was."

He smiled. "Does that mean I have beaten him out in your affections."

"The man's been dead for centuries. There was no contest."

He smoothed his finger across my cheekbones. "I love you so much," he said.

"I've been thinking the same thing about you," I returned shakily. "I just never thought you'd want to take me back with you to America, that you were afraid I wouldn't fit in." I bit my lip. "I probably won't, at first, but I'll try, Evan. I promise I'll try."

His whole face had become very still. "Are you saying you'd come to America with me?"

I said recklessly, "I'd go anyplace in the world if you were there."

This time his voice was shaky as he said, "Brave and gallant, as always. But you won't have to make such a sacrifice, my love. I have decided to remain in England and turn Stoverton into a profitable estate once more. I think my father would have wanted me to do that."

I sat up. "Are you serious? You're going to stay in England?"

"Yes. I didn't ask for it, but I have been entrusted with the lives of many people and I can't desert them. I've decided I shall just have to become the Earl of Althorpe and do my duty."

My mouth was hanging open. I had not expected this. "Are you sure?"

"Perfectly."

"It's not just because of me? It's what you really want to do?"

"Yes."

My heart lit like an explosion of candles. "Oh Evan, that makes me so happy!"

He gave me the sweetest, most tender smile. "I rather thought it would."

I lifted my arms to him and said, "Kiss me again!"

We kissed until we were both breathless and panting. Somehow we managed to shed our clothes and then we were truly close, skin against skin. I kissed him and kissed him, loving the feel of his strength, the feel of his flesh under my hands. He lowered his mouth to kiss my breasts and I gasped and arched up at the sharp sensation that went through my loins. He sucked on my nipple and I quivered, my body growing tauter and tauter, like a bow waiting to be shot. I opened my legs, feeling my need, wanting him to come into me.

When he did a hot drenching swell of pleasure came with him. I think I whimpered. I know I raised my hips so he could come even deeper. A shock of burning pain caused me to stiffen and cry out and he buried his face in my neck and said, "It will pass, Julia. It will pass." I hung onto him and let him stay, surrendering to him, feeling him inside of me, stretching me, giving me such mounting pleasure that I wanted to scream.

Then it happened, a fierce explosion of pleasure that caused my whole body to convulse, again and again and again. His seed poured into me and felt such exultation, such joy, that I thought I might die of it.

Evan turned me on my side and took me into his arms. "I love you so much," he kept saying. "So much."

"I love you more," I said, and he laughed.

*

We drove back to London the next day. Everyone crowded into the drawing room when they heard we had arrived, including Uncle Gordon, who had returned in my absence.

"Thank God you found her," Lady Barbara exclaimed.

Maria was hugging me so hard I almost couldn't breathe. "I'm sorry I worried you," I said. "I wasn't thinking very clearly."

"I know." Maria looked down at me, her blue eyes bright with unshed tears. "I know why you left, and I understand."

Lizzie came to hug me next. "I'm so glad to see you, Julia. You know how much I love you."

I did know and I was grateful for her love. Lizzie's friendship had been a great gift to me.

Aunt Barbara said ominously, "Where did you spend last night, Julia?"

It was Evan who answered. Clearly he thought himself a better liar than I was. "She stayed with Sir Matthew, Aunt, and I stayed at Stoverton."

Aunt Barbara fixed him with a piercing gaze. "Make sure that remains your story," she said.

My, my, I thought. Such a nasty mind.

"We are very happy to have you back," Uncle Gordon said, coming to kiss me on the cheek and to shake Evan's hand.

"I have put it about that you were ill," Aunt Barbara informed me. "Fortunately you were not gone for long. I think we shall muddle through all right. The marquis even asked about your health, Julia. I have hopes you can still attach him."

Evan and I looked at each other. I gave him a small nod and he took a deep breath and stepped forward. "I have some rather good news for you all. Julia has promised to become my wife." This brought gasps from all around. He continued, "And we plan to remain in England and live at Stoverton."

Dead silence greeted this part of the announcement. Lizzie recovered first, squealing and coming to hug me again. Then she hugged Evan. "This is wonderful! I have been praying it would happen – you two so clearly loved each other."

I looked at my cousin's beaming face. "How did you know *that*?"

"Oh, anyone with eyes could see it," she responded blithely.

Tears were rolling down Maria's face.

"Maria!" I said, rushing to her side. "What's wrong? Aren't you happy for us?"

She nodded, sniffled, and said, "I'm crying because I'm happy. I was so afraid I had lost you."

I wrapped her in my arms. "I would never desert you."

Evan said plaintively, "Don't I get a kiss, Maria? I'm going to be your brother now, you know."

She flew to him and kissed his cheek enthusiastically. "I'm so happy, Evan. So happy."

He grinned at her. "So am I."

Maria turned to me and said, "Just think, Julia, you'll be a Marshall after all! Think of all the family lore you can pass along to your children."

I blinked. Strangely, this thought hadn't yet occurred to me.

Uncle Gordon said, "This news calls for a celebration drink. Surely you have some champagne on ice, my dear?"

Lady Barbara looked doubtful.

Evan said, "I'm certain the estimable Grantly can come up with something."

Lady Barbara rang the bell.

Uncle Gordon said, "Come and sit down you two." When we obliged, he gave Evan an approving smile. "I'm delighted with your choice of bride and I'm delighted with your plan to remain in England. Stoverton needs a steady hand if it's to recover from the devastation of its previous owners."

Evan looked very serious. "That is the conclusion I came to myself." He turned to Aunt Barbara. "I believe this is what my father would have wanted me to do."

Aunt Barbara smiled. A real smile, not her usual pained one. "Dear Tommy. He did love Stoverton, you know. If only he had inherited instead of Philip this disaster would have been averted. I'm very glad his son has decided to take up the challenge."

"And Julia won't have to leave us and go to America," Lizzie said.

Evan said, "Chills run up and down my spine at the thought of Julia in Salem. The town would never recover."

"That's not true!" I said indignantly. "I told you I would go and do my very best to fit in."

"Well that's the strongest declaration of true love that I've ever heard," Lizzie said, smiling at me.

Uncle Gordon said, "Julia is not the only one to have marital news for us. I am pleased to inform you that Lizzie is to marry Lord Roger Ainsley, the Duke of Morton's brother."

"Lizzie!" I shrieked and went to hug her.

"She could have had the duke," Aunt Barbara said. "Instead she picks this young man who is going to be a **clergyman**."

"You picked me," Uncle Gordon reminded her. "What about that rich earl who wanted to marry you?"

We all stared at Aunt Barbara in amazement. To think someone else besides Uncle Gordon had wanted to marry her. It didn't seem possible.

"Well, it was you I loved, Gordon," Aunt Barbara said.

"Hah!" Lizzie grinned at her mother. "I believe that is how I told you I felt about Roger."

The door opened and Grantly appeared. "You rang, my lady?"

"Yes, Grantly, is it possible that we might have some champagne?"

"Of course, my lady. I always keep a bottle on ice in case it is wanted."

"Bring it up then, Grantly," Evan said. "We have something to celebrate today."

"Very good, my lord."

Grantly exited with his usual dignity and Evan said, "It seems there are some uses for a butler after all."

Aunt Barbara said with fervor, "Thank you, Evan, thank you for taking Julia off my hands."

There was a moment of startled silence, and then we all began to laugh. Evan put an arm around my shoulders and led me to one of the sofas. I sighed with deep satisfaction.

"I think Ty will be all the crack in the hunting field," I offered, thinking that perhaps we might even get to hunt with the Quorn if Tom could arrange it.

"Oh My God," Aunt Barbara said. "Does she never stop?"

I regarded the ring of amused faces looking at me. "What?" I said.

Evan dropped a kiss on the top of my head. "Pay no mind to them, my love. I'll always be interested in your hunting stories."

I gave him a radiant smile. God how I love that man. He said something to Uncle Gordon, and they fell into conversation. I leaned against him, happier than I had been in my entire life, and listened to the sound of his voice.

* * *

I love to hear from my readers. Feel free to email me at
joanemwolf@gmail.com.

CPSIA information can be obtained
at www.ICGtesting.com
Printed in the USA
BVHW032116100820
586079BV00001B/51

9 781949 135664